HIDDEN

A Novel

D1456494

Bea Klier

ISBN-10:1523430834

Published by Amazon.com (CreateSpace)

Dedicated to the memory

of my two beloved children,

Karen and Peter.

In dedicating this book to my children, I specifically am assigning all funds received, less publication costs, to the KAREN KIDDER LUNG CANCER RESEARCH FUND at the American Lung Association where Karen's foundation is housed. This includes any additional donations.

Prologue

They stood as if transfixed, brother and sister, slightly apart from one another, not touching, and a few inches away from the large dining room table that separated them from the heavyset youngish man standing opposite them. The man was about thirty-four, with a round handsome face, and the slightest trace of a nervous smile periodically creasing his cheeks. The boy who was the younger of the two by about five years was twelve. He looked at the man with a quizzical frown, sensing recognition, but not understanding his presence, and slightly irritated at having to cut short the softball game which his team was winning. He had responded to the call from the front steps of the apartment building by his mother and later by his sister, Belinda, whom he really wanted to call Belly, but settled for Betty. It was an unwritten rule that you are called twice, and after that you might relinquish some of your privileges, such as, playing ball after school, which to Henry were vital. It was summer, school was out and his life was predicated on softball.

Betty remembered this man well. He was her father--who had been kind and affectionate--and she always felt that she was special in his eyes. They had special private nicknames for one another, and she relished his attention. Her mother always seemed so preoccupied with her own thoughts that she didn't have time for the playful things, such as teasing, that the young girl needed. She was an attractive, intelligent and serious young woman who had graduated from secondary school this past winter and would enter the Free University in the fall. She really wanted to go to another school, but this was 1933 and there was barely enough money for food, rent and clothing for the three of them. In fact, Betty didn't know where the money came from to support them. She assumed that her father provided for them, even though he had not lived there with them for about four years.

She remembered her young growing years, when they had lived in opulence, in a private house with oriental rugs on the floor and velvet draperies on the windows and a long slinky black car parked elegantly in the driveway. She had pretty clothes. She remembered that Grandpa Linden, Daddy's pop, owned a dress factory, and he always had some of the operators in the shop make clothes for her. She remembered, with joy, the dark purple velvet coat with the grey squirrel collar and cuffs with a hat to match and a grey fur pompom to complete the outfit. This was her Easter outfit when she was twelve. She had been a bit of a snob then, because she had showed off her outfit to Harriet, her second cousin, who lived nearby and didn't have a Grandpa in the dress business. In fact, she didn't have a grandpa alive, when they were twelve. She suffered from a father who never provided adequately for his family. They were always considered the poor relatives, and everyone in the family treated them kindly, but Minna and Jack (Harriet's parents) never seemed content either with one another or with their status in life.

Betty felt that her Daddy seemed to be away from home a great deal, but he always returned with gifts, such as doll's clothing and colorful bracelets, and hugs and kisses. She always remembered how his rough beard scratched her face and Daddy always said that

6

someday she could tell her 'special feller' to shave more often, but that he preferred to shave once daily and that was enough. He would always wear perfectly pure white shirts, with a starched white handkerchief in the upper left pocket and the special ring on the pinky of his left hand, which always glistened in the light. Betty knew that he had been very sick and had to take special medicines. She always worried when he was away, but always knew that he would come back with his cheery, "Hi Boopsie,"

And, when…suddenly, he was not there, her life, she told her diary, went down the sewer.

///////////////

Chapter One
Brooklyn, 1914

It was a community where immigrants from Eastern Europe had settled. The Danvers had come from Eastern Europe in 1898 and had settled in Williamsburg, an area fairly close to the new Brooklyn Bridge cluttered with tenements (apartment houses) and some scattered town houses faced with brown stone, wide stairways to the street and iron railings which also enclosed the entry to a below-street-level tradesman's entrance. There were a few young trees dotting the sidewalks, which were narrow, as were the roadways, some still unpaved. The Danvers were affluent enough to own a four-storied brownstone building. Adjacent to the house were stables where Mr. Danvers kept his wagons and horses needed for his work. He was proud of his station in life, economically and socially. He was a wholesale fruitier. This meant that he had to be in the Wallabout Market at dawn to bid for the freshest fruits and vegetables which he then sold to the neighborhood grocery and fruit stores throughout the area. The women and men were out in the streets, standing at the stoops exchanging gossip. There were some pushcarts with produce, fish, scissor sharpeners and many with articles of clothing. The merchants who paid rent for stores did not like the pushcarts. The pushcart operators were poor immigrants trying to eke out a few dollars to support their families. There sometimes were severe arguments and the police would come at the behest of the store merchants and chase the carts away. Many of these families shared rooms and living conditions which were not much better than those hovels they had left in Europe or Ireland. But they had suffered deprivation, illness and loneliness to come to the Golden Land and they were not likely to give up now.

There also were street merchants who sold fresh vegetables and fruits from moveable pushcarts. These carts were a convenience for the housewives and domestic servants as they loudly hawked their wares. There also were independent fish peddlers, who would come around on Thursday and early Friday and they would shout, "F-i-sh F-r-esh F-i-i sh" and the women wiping their hands on their aprons, would scurry down to the street like the children responding to the Pied Piper. The women used this opportunity to gossip with one another, exchange recipes and note with disdain anyone who bought the less expensive fish.

Mr. Danvers hired several men to drive the horse-drawn wagons to go to the market as well as make the deliveries to the local stores. He was an austere man in his forties, tall and strait-laced, with an angular face, swarthy, and with the popular drooped moustache which made his appearance almost sinister. His nose was sharp, only softened by the clear blue eyes and the upward tilt of the lids which revealed the Asian influence of his forebears. He ruled his workers with the same discipline that he demanded from his family, such as the requirement to accept his word as the last word.

Claire, his beautiful young wife was not intimidated by his rigidity and brusqueness. She was a freethinker, as well as a free spirit. She was a good mother to her two children and a good wife, but she did not consider Morton's word as law. She felt that she had rights

9

and opinions which she could and should express on many matters. She felt that many of the traditions that kept women subservient to their husbands and fathers could be challenged. She took great pleasure in expressing her thoughts which sometimes annoyed and embarrassed Morton. He forgave her because he loved her dearly and quietly he admired her for her forthrightness and often proudly explained some of her arguments to other men. However, he never allowed the family or children to hear his support of those 'radical' ideas of Claire's. The comforts which he provided she accepted and enjoyed.... She loved good clothes, good food on the table and plenty of camaraderie with her friends and family. Her one indulgence after her family was her Tuesday morning with some ladies of similar status and interest, to play Whist.

This card game was very popular in the early 1900's and was a forerunner of Contract Bridge. She dressed carefully in the morning, piling her auburn hair high on her head and placed an amber hair ornament at the back of her coiffed head. Ana, the Polish maid, who did the cleaning, cooking and laundry in the house came to assist her in pulling the corsets on, giving her the classic hourglass figure showing off to great advantage the emerald green skirt, which fell softly to the ground. This day in early September required a high-necked long-sleeved lacy white silk for her 'going out' dress. A touch of rouge on her cheeks added to the glow which she emanated. Her high button shoes in white and the white stockings and beaded green bag almost completed the outfit. The elegant last touch was the hat and gloves. The hat was beige straw with green flowers and sat slightly forward on her forehead to give a modicum of shade. The white gloves with six buttons were ceremoniously put on and she said to Ana, "I'm ready. Call for the carriage."

As Claire descended slowly down the front stairs, she noticed her two friends, Celia and Sara, standing near the carriage with Oscar waiting patiently for the 'missus' to arrive. Claire greeted the women warmly, "How is everybody this morning?"

Each in turn responded, "We are just fine on this lovely day."

Oscar, properly removed his cap and nodded to Claire, who greeted him as well, "And how are you this lovely day?"

"I am well, missus."

"Let's go," Claire indicated as the women were assisted up into the carriage.

Oscar put his cap on and whispered to Claire, "Are we going to Miss Penny's?"

"Yes," Claire replied, as she joined her friends in the carriage.

In fact, these two women were not considered part of Claire's inner circle of friends. They simply were neighbors who liked to play Whist with her. If someone would have asked Claire how she made the distinction between these two neighbors and her "inner circle", she would have been hard pressed to give a rational answer.

The horses began their gallop down the street towards their destination, a short ten-minute drive to Penny's, really Penelope Smith, a true member of Claire's inner group. The sounds of the clip clop of the horses hooves on the pavement soon became less strident until silence prevailed and the sounds of the street and the early morning bustle of activity took over.

11

Chapter Two
The Danvers

The Danver's living space was the first three floors. The street floor entrance led to the kitchen, pantry and doorway for merchants to make deliveries. There was a large wooden table in the center of the large kitchen which was used by Ana and the wagon drivers who had their meals at the house. Ana had her own room just behind the kitchen and in a small vestibule there was a door and a few stairs leading to the garden at the back of the house. Often, the children, Stella, the eldest, and Ernst, her younger brother, would have their meals in the kitchen with Ana and the drivers. The next floor up the stairs was called the parlor floor because that room occupied almost half of the floor. It had the large bay window overlooking the street and was dark and usually kept closed. It had heavily upholstered chairs and a sofa, a dark maroon rug in the center, side tables with gas lamps, a fireplace with a metal framework and a mantel of wood. The fireplace was only used when the room was occupied by guests.

Behind the parlor was the formal dining room with its long rectangular table and eight high-backed chairs covered in burgundy velvet with tassels at each of their four corners. There was a crystal fruit bowl, always filled with the freshest seasonal fruits, in the center sitting on a lace runner covering the middle of the longer dimension. On the sideboard over which hung a long mirror in a gilded frame were two tall crystal candle sticks with another bowl, filled with nuts, centered on a similar lace runner. Against a small wall towards the rear of the room stood a serving cart on which was a collection of dried flowers, and on its lower shelf was the box of serving utensils. The silver service was in a locked drawer in the sideboard and the dishes were elegantly displayed in the china closet, which was against the opposite wall and had glass doors also locked. Behind the dining room, were stairways, one down to the kitchen and one up to the third level. In this hall there also was a dumbwaiter which brought the food up from the kitchen.

At the back of the house was another room, where Morton would sit after dinner and smoke his cigars and Claire would often sit and sew or read. Reading was not a major activity but they both liked to discuss the stories which were printed in the newspapers, as well as the local gossip and activities...Claire always had an opinion.

The third floor was the bedroom floor, where the Danvers family slept. The house had indoor plumbing, and in addition to the three bedrooms, there was another room called the sewing room, although little sewing took place there. The children used it as a playroom and Claire had a large walnut armoire with two heavy doors and a pullout drawer on the bottom, where she stored some out of-season clothing. There also was a low table with three mirrors which could be adjusted to see the sides of one's face, hair or hat and below there were a few small drawers, where hatpins, hairpins, combs, ribbons and other sundries were kept. Stella loved this room. Here she could preen in front of the mirror and fantasize her romantic dreams. Enjoyment was her major goal in life. All her needs were met, school, clothing food, home, so she was able to indulge her passion for fun! She had very few responsibilities, as Ana maintained the premises She also had the good fortune of having very few chores to perform at home as the two servants provided all the necessary cooking and cleaning that kept the household tidy and well-fed.

Claire had insisted that Morton buy a piano, because she felt that all young ladies should have a skill and Stella dutifully learned to play the pianoforte. She was moderately proficient in that she could read musical notation but with hardly any talent. Stella went to Girls High School which was a trolley ride away located in another community in Brooklyn. Several local young women made up their group. Stella was obviously the belle of the group as her father was a prosperous entrepreneur and above all she had her own pony and cart.

Ernst was a handsome young man and was a good student, who loved to read and dream. He was interested in what his father and the drivers did, so he stayed around the stables and chatted with the workers. He also learned a good deal about the business at a very young age. His father doted upon him and gave him as much attention as he, Morton, felt was warranted to a young 'snippet'. He constantly peppered Morton with questions on managing the workers' performance and keeping his customers happy.

This was a fairly ordinary family with fairly ordinary needs and no great crises other than planning the menu for dinner and cleaning the dirt off the tables in the parlor, or buying new antimacassars for the chairs when the whole family gathered for dinner. Claire was a gracious hostess and she loved having her mother, father, and Charles visit. She basked in the pride her parents showed at her successful marriage and family. From time to time she also entertained her other siblings, three sisters and two brothers, who were Ida, Lena, Minerva,

14

Benjamin, and Carl. The three sisters were married to hard-working men. For example, Ida was married to Jack and they owned a grocery store in an adjacent community. Benjamin and Carl were house painters. Although mother Rose was the matriarch of the family, Claire was the power behind the throne.

The fourth floor was occupied by Minerva, Claire's younger sister, and her husband, John. They had been married recently and as John was, in the language of the day, "not a good provider," Claire offered the top floor, and Morton reluctantly agreed. He was not a very charitable soul and especially did not find Min and John either very interesting or very worthy of his largesse. In truth, the marriage had been arranged by their mother, Rose, who found it intolerable that her youngest daughter had not found a husband at the advanced age of thirty. Min was a crotchety person, always whining and complaining to whomever would listen. The thought of sexual contact with a man was anathema to her pristine personality. In fact, Stella, who had been the flower girl at her wedding, accompanied them on their wedding journey to Niagara Falls. John was really a nice person. He rarely raised his voice or expressed dismay or anger towards Min for her complaining ways. He was tolerant of differences and accepted his lot in life. Albeit a meager provider, he would have probably been an accomplished linotyper today, but he rarely held a position for more than a few months.

/ / / / / / / / / / / / / / /

Chapter Three

Stella

It was a sunny Saturday morning when Stella came bouncing down the stairs, all decked out in a pale green georgette dress. Her thin face, with its enormous green eyes, was aglow with excitement. Her long brown hair flew out behind her as she bounded down the steps, shouting,

"Ana, Ana, look at this dress. Isn't it beautiful?"

"Of course," Ana agreed and tried to calm Stella down long enough to urge some breakfast. Stella sat down and started to eat and continued to babble with her mouth full.

"Oh, what a gorgeous day and today I am going to take Brownie out to visit Uncle Jack," Stella remarked defiantly. "I know the way and I want to have Papa understand that I am fifteen and old enough to hold the reins and get there and back by myself...I don't need Oscar to come with me all the time."

"I hope your Papa will agree, but I don't think so," Ana indicated.

At this juncture Claire entered the room. "What are you saying?" she queried.

"Oh! Mama, can I? Can I?" Stella pleaded?"

"What are you asking, child?

"I want to take Brownie and go visit Uncle Jack and Aunt Ida at the store and show them my new dress," Stella added.

"That is a very nice idea. Ask Papa and Oscar will go with you," Claire remarked.

"No. I don't want Oscar to come with me... I am not a baby!" Stella belligerently replied.

"We'll see," said Claire.

She turned to Ana and asked her to please call Oscar to come into the house. Stella was petulantly disturbed by this enforcement of parental authority. She resented any infringement of her rights, which she felt were inviolable.

Oscar, a thin reedy man of nondescript origin, came in, cap in hand and addressing Claire as Missus because he admired her very much, said, "What can I do for you?"

Claire indicated that Stella wanted to take the pony and cart out to visit her uncle. Oscar's eyes brightened and he said, "I'd be happy to drive the cart for Stella."

Stella responded angrily, "But I don't want you to come!"

Oscar continued, "Then you'd better come to the stable to speak to Mr. Dee."

Stella had stood waiting, and not too patiently, for her father in the stables as he was busy overseeing the veterinarian's care for the injury to one of the horses.

Noticing her standing off to one side instead of plunging in and asking questions he said, "I'll be with you in a minute, Stella."

Oscar was grooming her pony, Brownie, and she went to the stall to watch him.

"Oscar, will he, huh, will he?" Stella whimpered in a conspiratorial tone.

Oscar grimaced and shrugged his shoulders, not wanting to get involved in the family affairs. He was a quiet man, lived in a boarding house by himself. He had come to America as a young boy. He was shy and not very communicative. He was afraid of almost everything, except horses. He grew up on a farm near Lodz and he spoke of his home and family all the time. He was a lonely man. He felt comfortable and happy to work for Mr. Danvers and to be accepted into the family. He never shared much of his personal life or anything of his needs or interests. He was always kind and courteous to everyone. It was difficult to engage him in conversation. Only Stellie spoke to him as a friend. Even she in her flippant manner treated him as an underling sometime.

"All right, Stellie," Mr. Dee shouted. "Come into the office."

The office was about ten feet square just off to the end of the stable and had glass from the ceiling to about three feet from the floor and the rest was covered with boards that desperately needed painting. But as the appearance of the office added nothing to the profits derived from the business, he did not see any use for cosmetic change. Inside was a roll top desk, which was always locked. There was a small table and a few gnarled and worn chairs, also a cabinet with some papers. Most of the financial records were kept in the house. Even though the desk was locked, as was the office, he did not trust his workers and wanted no one snooping around.

Stella, although resigned to her fate, heaved a mournful sigh, her face becoming distorted, she angrily replied, "I still think I can manage Brownie by myself," and ran out of the office.

A grin crossed his face; he shook his head and muttered, "That girl has a bit of the devil in her."

Controlling her tears and her anger she ran to her room and

changed into her going-out clothes. Oscar had the pony cart ready for her in front of the house. He wore his cap and doffed it ceremoniously as Stella climbed into the cart.

"Where to today, Princess? Are you going to visit JP Morgan or the Rothschild's?"

Stella was angry, but couldn't help laughing at this joke, which they shared each time they went for a ride.

Stella had a long neck and she carried her head high and acted as if she were the princess she'd read about in a book once. She looked around her as Oscar led the way to her friend Amy's house trying to catch the eye of anyone whom she might recognize, so that they could see Stella Danvers out for a ride in her very own cart.

"Whoa, Brownie, here we are. Do you want me to call Amy?" Oscar said.

"No, I'll go," she replied.

She ran up to Amy's house which was on the second floor of a fairly decent looking tenement. Amy was totally intimidated by Stella. Although she could rarely resist any of her suggestions, they really depended upon one another. It was a genuine symbiosis, but this time Stella was disappointed. Amy's mother would not let her out because she felt feverish. There was so much talk about this new cold called influenza, that everyone feared it. Mrs. Roth would not let Stella into the house, and Stella left.

Returning to the cart, Stella said to Oscar, "Let's go to Uncle Jack's store. You can go away for an hour, because I'm going to visit with them for a while."

/ / / / / / / / / / / / / / / /

19

Chapter Four

Martin

Martin lived in a tenement house some ten to fifteen blocks away and this family, the Larkin's, was sitting down to breakfast. The family was Papa (Sidney), Mama (Rachel) and Martin with his two sisters. Mama was round and cherubic. Papa was tall husky and gentle. They were having a difficult time keeping themselves in a modest economic state. Papa worked as a cutter in a sweat shop in Brooklyn. Janine, the eldest, worked as a sewing operator in the same shop as Papa. Eva, the younger sister, was musically talented and worked a few nights each week at the local cinema playing the piano. Martin was still a student at Boys High School. He was fifteen.

"So what do you plan to do today, Marty?" Papa said.

"Oh, Papa, didn't Mama tell you? I have a job," Martin said proudly.

"Where? How did you get it?" Papa continued.

"I was walking home with Rudy and he lives over near Marcy Ave. So I walked home with him. We passed this grocery store and there was a sign in the window which said 'Boy Wanted', so I went in, and Mr. Albert, he's the owner of the store, said I could work there after school and on Saturdays. I was so excited I ran all the way home and told Mama. I thought she told you!" Marty explained.

Papa rose from his chair and walked over to Marty and kissed him on his cheek.

"Why did you do that?" Marty said. He rubbed his cheek in

embarrassment.

"You are my son and I am proud of you. You took a responsibility all by yourself and that is good. Mama did tell me, but I wanted to hear it from you," Papa explained.

Martin raised his eyebrows questioning this statement, but suddenly realized that he had to leave to get to the store. He jumped up and said bye and went over to kiss Mama before he ran out of the door. Martin raced down the four flights of steps and into the street, greeting some of the young boys playing cards in the empty lot next to the building on Boerum Street. He was happy and excited at the prospect of working and bringing home the dollar he was promised. He envisioned twenty things he could get for that money, but knew that Mama needed it and that dimmed his visions of new socks or knickers or of even a book on how things work. He was fascinated by machines and their mechanical structure. Although working in a grocery was not his goal, he saw this as a golden opportunity to convince Mama and Papa to let him finish high school and go to some kind of a trade school. He ran most of the way and stopped at the street before the grocery to smooth his dark brown hair and catch his breath.

Chapter Five

The Meeting

"Good Morning, Mr. Albert, Mrs. Albert," Marty said.

"Oh! Marty, hello. How are your Mama and Papa today?" Mrs. Albert asked.

"Oh, they are just fine, thank you," Marty answered.

Mr. Albert indicated the white apron which Marty ceremoniously put on, feeling very grown up and 'in charge'.

"Today, you are going to work in the back room where all the boxes and cartons are," said Mr. Albert. "I want you to make some order out of the mess. I'll come back later to see how you're doing. Any questions, just let me know. All right?"

Marty left and went to the back room.

"Jack," Ida called, "Come here! Mrs. Feinstein has a problem. She said that yesterday she bought two pounds of cornmeal, but when she brought the bag home she weighed it and it was only one pound and a half."

Jack was angry, but restrained his temper because Mrs. Feinstein was a good customer and did not 'put it on the bill' as so many of the families did and paid what they could at the end of the week or month.

"No problem, go to the barrel and take another half pound," Jack answered.

She haughtily turned on her heel and went to the barrel and scooped some cornmeal into a paper bag. She was disappointed that

Mr. Albert agreed so readily because she wanted to make him uncomfortable. She did not like him because he would not respond to her obvious flirtatious manner, when Ida (Mrs. Albert) was not in the store.

"Is this the right amount?" Mrs. Feinstein asked as she gingerly held the bag for him to weigh.

Jack replied, "That's just fine and enjoy your bread making. Have a good Saturday."

Jack then bent down to retrieve something from the counter and motioned silently to Ida to enquire if Mrs. Feinstein had left. He heard the bell ring on the door and then stood up.

"I don't know why she is the only person who gets short weights," Jack remarked.

"Oh Jack, don't fuss, she just loves you, that's all." Ida teased and patted him affectionately.

"Ida, what are you saying?" Jack asked.

"Never you mind, I can see the lust in her eyes," Ida continued.

"Hush! There's a young boy in the back," Jack whispered.

Ida laughed and Jack joined in.

Ida and Jack lived upstairs in a small apartment and Ida was pregnant and expecting her first child. Jack was worried that she stood on her feet too much and was hoping that the young boy they had hired would be available when Ida had to give birth. The store was busy with shoppers and it was soon time for Ida to rest and have a cup of tea, which they both liked. While they were sipping their tea, the door was flung open and Ida exclaimed, "Why darling, Stella, how good to see you! "

As Stella entered the store she fussed with her dress and hair, wanting to make the very best impression. Jack and Ida were very fond of their niece. They admired her energy and her willingness to stand up to her father, who was not among their favored relatives.

"Stellie, you look beautiful today. Is that a new dress?" Ida said admiringly.

"Yes," Stella said. "Mama and I went shopping at Namms on Fulton Street and we bought this."

"That color is so pretty. It makes your eyes look so blue."

"Auntie you know that my eyes are green," Stella replied. "How could they turn blue?"

"Excuse me a minute, Stellie," Ida interrupted. There is a man whom we have to talk to."

"Why don't you go in the back?" Jack said. "There is a mirror there and see if your eyes didn't turn blue!"

As Stella slowly sauntered to the back of the store, she opened one of the penny candy jars and took out a few jelly beans. She could hardly get the door open, because there was something in the way, so she started to push the door, when a voice said,   "Just a minute, Mr. Albert. I'll move the carton," Martin called.

"Who are you and what are you doing in this room?" Stella imperiously asked the man.

"Oh, I'm sorry," Martin sheepishly responded. "I thought it was Mr. Albert."

"No, it isn't. It's his niece, Stella."

"Oh, I'm sorry, Miss," Martin said apologetically.

"Well, who are you?"

"My name is Martin, and I work here. "

"I didn't know Uncle Jack had anyone working for him," said Stella blushing.

"Well, today is my first day."

"Oh, pleased to meet you," as she extended her hand forgetting the jelly beans. The candy scattered onto the floor and they both laughed nervously.

"Do you go to school?" Stella inquired.

"Of course," Martin replied. "I'm at Boys High."

"Well, I'm at Girl's High. How often do you work here?"

"I work every day after school and on Saturdays," Martin replied proudly.

"When do you have time for yourself?" Stella questioned.

"I don't think about it," Marty said. "It is important to work and besides, we can use the money."

"Where is the mirror?" Stella asked.

"The mirror? I don't know," he answered.

"Well, they said it was here. Let's look," Stella said.

The mirror turned out to be in a corner where the cartons were and Stella tried to squeeze into the space, when Martin, trying to make room for her, put his arm on her shoulder to move her closer to the mirror. He removed his hand quickly, but in that instant Stella looked up at him and caught his eye.

"See, my eyes are not blue. They are green. Look."

Martin very shyly looked at her face and said, "You have eyes that are called hazel and they sometimes do change color."

"Well, nice to meet you," and she returned to the front of the store emotionally a bit distressed.

"Did you meet Martin?" Ida asked when Stella regained her composure.

"Uh huh."

"He is a very nice boy from a very nice family."

"What is that to me? He's a grocery boy." Stella said huffily. "Someday, I will marry a very rich man and leave Brooklyn and live in the country where I will have many servants, horses, and lots of money to buy anything I want."

"I hope you get your wish," Ida said quietly.

After some general conversation about the family, Oscar walked in and as it wasn't   like Stella to be quiet ever, he asked, "Are you all right, Miss Stella?"

"I'm just fine" Stella said soberly.

She was particularly quiet on the short ride home. Oscar recognizing her silence, did not disturb her. When they reached the stable, she leaped out of the cart and ran into the house and up the stairs and sat at her table to look in the mirror. She thought: *He said my eyes were hazel. I never heard that. He is so handsome and so strong. My heart is jumping up and down and I can't stop thinking about his hand on my shoulder. I feel really strange. Oh, I wish Amy wasn't sick so I could talk to her. Maybe tomorrow, I'll get her to come with me to the store and see what I'm talking about. Oh no! Tomorrow is Sunday and the store is closed. I'll have to wait until Monday.*

/ / / / / / / / / / / / / / / /

Chapter Six

Thoughts

Although Martin was not normally shy among girls his own age, he was surprised how he had reacted to this girl, Stella. He thought, *She was not the prettiest girl, but she was fiery. Yeah, that's the word fiery. Full of fire, just the way she walked and carried her head so high on her neck, someone really different. I guess maybe rich girls are like that. Never knew one before.*

He finished sorting the cartons and sat down to eat the sandwich his Mama had made for him. Mr. Albert made him a cup of tea, and he sat among the boxes thinking about the girl and whether he would ever see her again. *No matter*, he thought, *I have other things to worry about. School, the books I need to buy for machines and how they work, and the good stories Papa can tell about the old country.* He was not unhappy; he just wished he had more of the things that a few dollars would buy. War talk was in the papers. He liked to look at the 'Brooklyn Eagle' and read it when Papa brought it home from the shop. *Would I become a soldier when I am older?* Martin thought. *I guess I would have to go if they called me. I will not go voluntarily.* He loved this country, but he had other plans for himself and that did not include a stint in the army.

He had great faith in the 'gold in the streets' myth that had been foisted upon new immigrant families. Since the 1880's, as industrialization in the US became the overwhelming economic direction, the need for low-entry-level workers became an urgency. As unsettling conditions existed in Czarist Russia with its militarism

27

and disdain for the poor, the prevalent anti-Semitism and the need to avoid military service, thousands of Russians, Jews and Christians alike, from the Ukraine and elsewhere, where food was at a premium and conditions were feudal, many of these families began the exodus to the 'new country'. Many were unskilled. Many were farmers with no concept of urban life. Others had only the few skills needed to survive in the 'old country'. This need for change and the possible 'gold in the streets' phenomenon, spread to many other countries where conditions were not much better, e.g., Austria, the Balkans, Germany, and Italy. In Italy, the propaganda called for heavy industrial workers to work in America's mines, railroads, steel, and the beginnings of the auto industry. Many thousands of families trekked westward, via many circuitous routes. Crushed in the holds of the ships with little space for a semblance of civilized life, these hardy pioneers landed in Ellis Island and many remained to struggle for existence in New York City.

These families put down roots and their children only understood the deprivation of their parent's emigration by frequent stories of the old country. Martin loved those stories and he never tired of them. He dreamed of visiting those places. He dreamed of wealth. He dreamed of living in a fine house with carpets and draperies. He wanted so much more than he had and so much more than he saw on the horizon. So he continued to dream...

/ / / / / / / / / / / / / / /

Chapter Seven

Phone Call

Stella had a difficult time keeping her mind on her school work. Clare, her mother, wanted to discuss with her the plans for a family party, which would take place the following week. Stella usually liked to fuss with these things, but this time her mind seemed to be preoccupied with other thoughts. She busied herself in her room, fussing with her long hair which she still wore loosely tied back at the base of her neck and she brushed it sensually as it cascaded down her back in ripples of dark brown waves. She kept looking in the mirror trying to fathom these strange emotions which seemed to engulf her very being for the last week. She knew silently what was happening, and she was frightened. She didn't quite understand the difference between lust and love, but the images danced in her head and she was in a quandary as to how the feelings could be hidden or contained. Yet the stress of dealing with these feelings was so overwhelming, she knew that she had to devise some plan to relieve the tension as well as keep all this pain locked up in her head so that her family would not have a clue. Although only fifteen, she was wise and headstrong. She knew she could easily play the part of an obedient daughter and satisfy all the familial responsibilities, while rummaging through her 'bag of tricks' to make some arrangement to see Martin alone.

The kitchen was busy with Claire and the housekeeper discussing the menu for the party next week.

"Oh, Stellie, what do you think?" Clare asked. "Should we have roast turkey or chicken? Which do you think would be better?"

"Mama, I think chickens would be better," Stella maturely responded. "You know how Grandma sometimes makes a funny face when we talk about roast turkeys!"

"Yes, you are absolutely right," Clare answered. "You are always so aware of the family and so helpful. Thank you. I think we have all the rest planned. We'll bake some cakes and pies and some fresh bread. Which tablecloth should we use?" Clare added.

Stella thought a moment and said, "I love the one with the lace cutouts on the edges. I think that would be very pretty with the pale blue edging on the dishes."

"Well, I guess that's it. Will you write up the list of people and then we will ask Papa to use the telephone to call some and then we can send the invitations to the rest," Clare remarked.

Stella began to leave the warmth of the kitchen, which she was loathe to do, but knew she had to spend some time thinking.

Mama said, "It's all right, darling. I don't need you anymore. We will finish by ourselves."

Behind the house there was a small garden which ran behind the barn as well. When Stella was younger she used to play there with her friends. It was fairly secluded and only one or two windows on each floor faced to the rear. She went there and sat on a wooden swing and tried to resolve her problem. No magic bullet came to her. She was unable to focus on the problem. She wished she could talk to someone. She had to talk to someone. *It had to be Martin, but how?* Stella thought. Suddenly, Papa called to her and said to come into his office quickly. She ran around the back of the barn and through the large doors facing the street.

"Yes, Papa, what do you want?" Stella said.

"There is someone who wishes to talk to you personally," her father said.

"Me?" Stella questioned.

It was an event to talk on the phone, and she usually didn't know too many children who had phones. Gingerly, she picked up the earpiece and held the other part of the instrument in her other hand and hesitantly said, "...er, hello!"

"Is this Stella?" the caller said.

"Yes. Who is this?" Stella responded.

"I don't know if you remember me, but my name is Martin, and you met me at your Uncle Jack's store last week."

Stella's hands began to tremble, and she felt almost faint and had to grab the edge of the desk for support.

"Oh, yes, I remember you," Stella said. "How are you?"

"Well," Martin said. "I don't have much time. I asked Jack, excuse me, Mr. Albert, if I could call you, because I needed to ask you something."

"Sure," Stella said. "What do you want?"

At this point, this entire incident caused Stella to wonder what her father's reaction had been when Martin made this unexpected telephone call. In this case she assumed correctly, that her Uncle Jack Albert had reassured Stella's father that Martin was working at the store. Jack told Morton that Martin was a reliable and trustworthy young man.

Martin then said, "Well, my school is having a dance this Friday night, and I wondered if you would be able to go with me. I

31

won't be able to come to your house, because I have to work after school, and I wouldn't have time."

Stella was so overcome by the invitation, but was unwilling to show her excitement. She was silent for a moment and Martin said, "I hope it is all right to ask you. Your Uncle Jack said he would tell your parents that it was all right for you to go -- that is, if you want to."

Finally, back in control of her voice, she said so politely, "I think that is a very nice idea. I will get the groom to drive me to your school. What time?" Stella asked.

"Can you be there by six o'clock? There will be food - not much - but if your parents want you to eat dinner, I guess you could come later," Martin said.

"No, no, six o'clock will be fine. I will tell my Papa to have me picked up by nine and we can then drive you home, too!" Stella announced.

"Oh, that would be just wonderful," Martin exclaimed. "I am so happy that you can come."

"Me too. See you Friday," Stella replied hanging up the telephone.

Stella needed to escape somewhere by herself quickly to savor this unbelievable piece of joy, but she had to explain to Papa who was standing nearby in the office that she had met this boy at Uncle Jack's store and was impressed at how courteous he was, and that Uncle Jack and Aunt Ida thought so, too. She watched Papa's face and by her clever description of Martin's demeanor, she had neutralized her father once again.

/ / / / / / / / / / / / / / /

Chapter Eight
The Dance

Stella ran around to the back again, but the swing was not enough to hold her. She had to run, share the excitement somehow, somewhere. Amy lived too far away, and she wouldn't understand. No, there were none among her friends who would feel what she was feeling and be supportive. This was something she just had to enjoy by herself. And so began a path from which she hardly deviated for the rest of her life. Very few would share her thoughts and feelings. Very few would ever know what her feelings were, and if this self-containment required it, she would lie to protect herself.

In the meantime, the preparations continued in the kitchen, and the wonderful aroma of food cooking distracted Stella enough for her to calm down and deal with her everyday activities.

Friday night soon arrived, and she told no one at school that she was going to a party with Martin. She didn't share this news with Amy, as she knew that she would be bursting with excitement and she didn't want Amy to know how she really felt. Stella always assumed that her thoughts, emotions, and actions were more mature or grownup than those of her friends. Although she relished her friendships, she did not feel comfortable sharing these serious private thoughts with anyone.

She dressed very carefully wearing a new bright blue dress that had many petticoats. She brushed her hair until her scalp hurt. It was quite long and very dark brown. She wore it hanging loosely down her back and merely clasped with an amber barrette, which her mother had bought for her last year. Her fair skin, dotted with freckles was a sharp contrast to her dark hair and bright eyes. She came down for the approval of her family and, of course, her mother, Claire, was ecstatic. Her father was less effusive, but secretly adored and admired her. Stella glowed in the aura of these expressions of love and admiration.

Oscar and Stella went by pony cart to the school, and despite her bravado, Stella was quite shy in a new surrounding and went sheepishly into the gymnasium which had already begun to be crowded with young people, all happy and laughing. She wandered to the food tables and took a small chicken salad sandwich to eat. Someone offered her a cup of punch and she was finding it difficult to swallow. She found a seat near a girl all in pink and ate her little sandwich. She worried that Martin would not remember her, but she was sure to recognize him. She gazed intently at the door, hoping she would not miss his entrance.

"Oh, there he is!" she gasped silently. She placed the food on the chair and jostled her way to the door and greeted him warmly.

Martin was taken aback at her appearance and said stumbling, "Golly, you look beautiful."

They danced and talked to his friends and Stella was so happy to be seen with this handsome boy.

Martin turned to Stella and said, "Can I see you next week? You see, Jack, Mr. Albert, is going to Port Chester for two days to visit his sister who is not very well, and he will keep the store closed, but he wants me to come in for a little while each day to do some cleaning up."

"Of course," Stella exclaimed. "I'd be happy to."

Wednesday came and Stella told her family that she was going with Amy after school to shop on Fulton Street and that she would be home for dinner.

/ / / / / / / / / / / / / / /

Chapter Nine

Intimacy

Stella knocked on the door of the store and Martin came and greeted her warmly. She went into the back and watched him as he worked.

He said, "You will have to get up off the box, because I have to move it."

"I dare you to lift me off it," Stella taunted. "I bet you can't lift me."

"Of course I can," he boasted. "You are light as a bird."

He approached her, grabbed her around her back and under her knees and lifted her effortlessly. In a surge of emotion, Stella grabbed him around the neck and kissed him fully on the mouth. He excitedly kissed her passionately, placing her carefully on a mat on the floor.

"Ooh, Stella you are so wonderful. I think about you all the time."

"Me too," Stella exclaimed breathlessly as they began to tear at their clothes until Martin was caressing her naked body and she his. It wasn't long before he penetrated her and they both were ecstatic in the release of their passion.

"Oh, Martin, what have we done?"

"It's OK," Martin said. "Was this the first time?"

"Yes," said Stella, and you?"

"Martin sheepishly said: "No, it wasn't."

They then dressed and were embarrassed and turned away from

each other--but Martin came up behind Stella and whispered, "I love you, and I think I always will."

Stella did not reply at once, as the reality of the situation suddenly became evident. He was not in her long-range plan, but he made her feel so good.

And after a few seconds she too exclaimed, "I love you, too!"

They tried to see one another as often as possible during the next few weeks, but Stella never invited him to her home. The only time any one at home saw him was at Jack's store.

Suddenly, Stella knew that something was wrong. She had missed her menstrual period. She thought she would wait a little longer and see if it came on, but it didn't. She went in a panic to Martin and told him. He was upset at this turn of events and really didn't know what to do. Stella decided that she must tell her mother and that her parents would do something.

Of course, Stella's mother, Claire, was horrified that her Stella could be in such a situation and how to tell her husband. The two families would have to meet and find a solution to these new circumstances.

When the Larkins arrived one evening with Martin, the atmosphere resembled a wake. All seemed unhappy at the situation they all faced. As abortion was not a consideration, the only alternative was marriage, and immediately. Martin and Stella hardly spoke to one another, but managed to find a moment alone in another room in the house.

Martin said, "I don't care, I love you and we will find a way out."

Stella said the same, but was saddened to think that her youth was over and now she would be a woman, a state of life she had not anticipated to come for many years. All of her fantasies, all of her plans were destroyed. She knew that there was no one to blame but herself and she had to accept that. Martin also was aware that his dreams would never be realized and that he would have to leave school and find a job.

Within a few weeks, Claire had announced to the family that Stella and Martin were engaged and would be married very shortly and would live on the third floor of the house, which was being renovated. Martin would then go to work for Papa as a mechanic and everything would work out just fine.

The families and friends knew that this was a "shotgun" wedding, and even though no one ever mentioned it, everyone knew. Of course, the Larkins were angry and distraught and naturally blamed that 'hussy' for all the troubles.

The wedding took place at the Danvers' house, a very quiet event, with just the immediate families and a few of Stella and Martin's friends. The newly married couple went to the St. George Hotel for two nights for a honeymoon. Stella tried to make Martin laugh, but she rarely succeeded. They both cried, but still clung to each other in their predicament.

On June 6, 1917, a girl, Betty, was born to the new sixteen year old parents. Although the birth of the child was a joy to all concerned, the parents and both sets of grandparents felt the sadness behind the joy. Martin hated to be beholden to Morton for his sustenance and Stella was unhappy still living in her parents' home. Although the relationship between Stella and Martin seemed stable, there were rippling undercurrents of sadness, anger, and despondency. Both Stella and Martin tried to maintain a fairly pleasant comforting environment for their child in which to grow and develop. Each took unusual pride and wonderment at this product of their love, Martin especially. Martin was an unusual father. He would spend as much time as he could spare with Betty, whom he affectionately called *Boopsy*. Stella seemed a bit more distant, but had deep feelings for this child. Because three generations were living in close proximity, Betty developed very quickly into a wise little girl.

/ / / / / / / / / / / / / /

Chapter Ten
Rockaway

Morton Danvers had been disappointed in the way Brooklyn was developing. He felt that the availability of new markets was not forthcoming. He realized that Queens County offered a better place for his entrepreneurship. It was a growing community and now that he had converted his horse-drawn carts to trucks, he could get to the markets quicker. He purchased a building in Rockaway, which was an oceanside community where real estate was booming and space was available. The building he had purchased had separate apartments on the second and third floors and the street floor was used as the office for the Danvers Produce Company with space adjoining the building for the trucks.

On a sunny morning in May, Betty and her friend, Marjorie, who was smaller and, although the same age as Betty, was shy and quiet, while Betty was very sure of herself, and, as she was fussed over a great deal, she was a little self-centered. Betty's Daddy, Martin, was delighted with Boopsy. Sometimes, he called her *Admiration*, because she had chubby cheeks and resembled the advertisement for Admiration Cigars which Martin liked to smoke. This morning, Claire came to the two girls and took a crate and sat down with them.

"And what are you ladies planning to do today?" Claire inquired.

"Oh, Grandma," Betty responded, "We are not ladies; we are girls."

"Well, girls can be ladies by the way they act," said Claire.

Marjorie asked, "Could you tell us a story before you go? My Grandma is always busy washing and cleaning and cooking and never tells us stories, but Betty is so lucky because you are always dressed and going out."

"Thank you dear," Claire responded. "That is very kind of you, but you must remember to love your grandma also. Well, let me see. There once was a little girl who was to meet her aunt at the train station. She comes to the train and sees a lady get off and she begins to run towards her, when suddenly another lady looking exactly like her aunt comes down from another car, then another, and another until there are many, many ladies all looking like her aunt. She doesn't know what to do, when suddenly a man comes up to her and asks what is the matter and she cries that she cannot find her aunt, that all the women look alike. He asks her if she know why they all look alike and she doesn't know.

He sits her down and says, 'This is just a way to show you how sad it would be if we were all alike. Don't you think it is better that we are all different?'

'Oh yes, I do. I know why I couldn't find her. I did a bad thing at home,' remarked Marjorie. 'I had wished that everyone was like me and that people with different colors and different shaped eyes were not as good as I was.' Suddenly she looked at the platform and all the women had changed. They all were different, except one who was her Aunt Letty. Now that is the story for today."

"Thank you. We understand what you mean."

Betty turned to Claire and said, "Where are you going today?"

41

"Betty, you know that today is Tuesday and I go to play Whist with my friends. I also go on Thursdays." Claire stood up and kissed Betty and Marjorie and said, "Good-bye ladies." She turned and left.

/ / / / / / / / / / / / / /

Chapter Eleven
The Marriage

Adjacent to the building was a large open field. Here, the trucks were parked and behind the field was another building which was a sort of barn/garage, where Martin kept his tools and where he serviced the trucks. He was a good mechanic, but felt it was demeaning. He had resigned himself to the work and to the fact that he was now a father and a husband and he plodded along each day. However, he was especially delighted with his daughter. Stella and he were tolerant of one another and kept up the pretense of a loving couple, but there was much bitterness between them. He was civil and sometimes loving. He knew that if it weren't for Betty, life would be intolerable. To add to the complexity of their lives, Stella was now pregnant again.

She decided that perhaps this would be a way to hold Martin closer. She still loved him and he loved her, but the circumstances of their marriage did not make for real happiness, as both of their goals had been aborted by one foolish and careless afternoon. They never spoke of that experience. They had their life together and they made it work by small increments of joy. Betty was such a delight and to both of them, such a miraculous event, that Stella felt another child and maybe a boy would make Martin happier.

In September, Betty was registered in a local elementary school. As there was no kindergarten, she entered first grade as the youngest child in the school. She was assigned to the first row, third seat. One morning, during the first weeks in school, the class was practicing penmanship. Betty, who already knew her letters and numbers and could write, took her pencil in her left hand and began to scribe the circles and slants to the cadence enunciated by Ms. Hagerty. "Round and round we go, and up and down we go. Lift round we go!" The door opened and in walked the principal, Miss Marsh. She walked up the first aisle, next to the wardrobe and stopped at Betty's desk.

"What are you doing, child?" she demanded.

"I'm writing," said Betty without lifting her head.

"Miss Hagerty, this child must be taught to write properly," and she pulled the pencil from Betty's hand and placed it in her right hand.

Thence began a struggle as Betty pulled the pencil out and replaced it in her left hand. After a while, she was in tears and the teacher and principal were *tsk tsking* in the front of the room.

Betty ran to her home, just a few streets away, and burst into the kitchen spilling out her tale of woe.

Stella, only twenty-one years old herself, and very mindful of authority, told Betty, "What the teacher says, you must do."

Betty shouted in anger, "Why don't you go and tell the teacher I write with my left hand."

Stella answered, "Rules are rules."

For all of her future academic life, she always maintained a distance from teachers -- was obedient and rigidly followed the rules. She later would say that she never left the room to go to the bathroom, even in high school and college, because she did not want to incur the wrath of the teachers. Only at home and with friends was she more outgoing.

In January of the next year, her brother was born, a beautiful blonde cherub, a wonderful combination of both of his handsome parents. They called him Henry.

The years flew by, with very little change in the marriage. Martin was a good father to both of the children and Stella provided the home with care and love. When Betty was nine and Henry four years old, a major tragedy befell the family. Claire, who had a history of a mild cardiac condition, was working in the office on the street floor, helping with the accounts. It was a cold wintry January day and with the door opening into the street, she felt the cold more so, as the drivers and other business people entered the office. She placed a gas heater near the door and put a chair near the door so that those entering would have to push the door slowly, reducing the loss of heat. One of the drivers came barging in a huff and left the door open for a few moments while explaining a problem to Claire. She asked him to please close the door firmly, and she got up to put the chair against the door. She went about her business, felt light-headed, fainted, and fell off the chair onto the floor. She remained there about twenty minutes.

Then suddenly Martin could be heard shouting, "Open the door, Mom, please," but there was no response.

He went to the window and saw her on the floor. He got a hammer, broke the window on the door, pushed the chair away and burst into the room with a handkerchief over his nose. The heater's gas flame had been blown out by a gust of wind and Claire was overcome. They could not revive her. She was forty-six years old.

45

(Accident #1)

The sadness that befell the household and the community was overwhelming. Stella and Betty felt the loss most severely. Stella had lost her mother, friend, and confidante. Betty, most of all, lost the one person who had loved her unconditionally.

Claire's husband suffered as well. His loss was translated into bitterness, anger, and rigidity in all social relationships. Martin felt the brunt of his anger and found working with Morton almost intolerable. Morton, on the other hand, found no comfort with the family at all. He began to leave the house after work hours and returned late at night. He would go to the local civic center where the business men gathered to chat and play cards. Tensions began to develop amongst the family's adults.

At the same time, Ernst, Stella's younger brother, who, although he was always quiet and unassuming, was happy to just be of help to Morton. Ernst had grown into a handsome young man and was interested in the business which his father willingly shared with him. Stella felt that she was sitting on a bubble that was to burst soon. She was too young and inexperienced to know how to manage the three men and the two young children in her care.

/ / / / / / / / / / / / / / /

Chapter Twelve
Accident #2

One day, two years after Claire's death, Martin was fixing the brake pedal on one of the larger Mack trucks which were now part of a fleet of trucks in the yard. At that time there was a very high step, which was the only way to enter the cab of the truck. Martin had a helper who was standing nearby to hand him the tools he needed. He had one foot on the high step and was kneeling with the other on the floor of the cab trying to fix the pedal, when suddenly the helper shouted to Martin, and as he turned, his foot slipped off the step and he fell to the ground with one leg pinned beneath him.

He tried to stand and realized that he could not. The helper ran to the phone and called for an ambulance, and Martin was rushed to Far Rockaway Hospital.

The doctors said that the patella on his right knee was fractured and needed surgery at once. Martin refused to be treated at that hospital, because he did not feel that the physicians were competent. He remembered that his sister Evelyn's husband, Joseph, had a bone injury some time before and had gone to a specialist. Stella called Evelyn explaining why Martin needed a specialist.

Evelyn suggested that Martin come by ambulance to the Orthopedic Hospital in Manhattan. She said she would pay for the transfer. Dr. Albee, a noted orthopedic surgeon at the time, performed the required surgery. Stella couldn't visit Martin frequently in Manhattan as the trip from Rockaway to the hospital was a long one.

This allowed his visitors to be mostly from his family as they all lived in Brooklyn, a closer ride to Manhattan. Stella was not happy about Martin's interaction with his family rather than with her and wondered what they had to say to one another. She always had questions about the honest intentions of his clan.

/ / / / / / / / / / / / / / /

Chapter Thirteen
The Hospital

Evelyn, Martin's middle sister had met Joseph, a rather unattractive small man with large ears and nearsighted eyes behind thick glasses, in the movie house where she played the piano. He was very bright and was a graduate of City College with a degree in Chemistry. He already had started a business and was earning a sizeable income. Evelyn, who was a beautiful woman, was attracted to this young man. No one else could fathom why, but she loved him and they married. Their first child Lucille was born, a year after Stella's son, Henry.

Very early in Joe and Ev's marriage, it became apparent that the roles that each would play began to be established. Ev was the beautiful caring woman, who rarely spoke if Joseph was around. He soon became not only the master of his own household, but began to take on the role of patriarch of the entire family. When any decisions had to be made, he was consulted and usually his advice was taken.

In the year after Eva and Joe married, Martin's older sister, Janette, married, by contrast, a tall handsome young man called Murray, who was already associated with a large manufacturing firm of optical instruments and equipment. He was a quiet serious person, never raised his voice and was generous and caring to his family. He quickly rose in the ranks of the firm to become Vice President of Sales. There is no doubt how absolutely delighted Martin's parents were of the successful marriages of both of their daughters. They were grieved by the life which their only son was forced (their words) to endure. Why this attractive bright star was denied the opportunity they were more than willing to provide, to "be somebody" and instead was a father at sixteen and worked in a dead-end job for a man they all disliked intensely. They loved his children and doted on Betty, but for Stella, there was only cold acceptance, as the mother of Martin's children.

This antipathy was never overtly expressed by any of Martin's family. They were socially correct and were polite and gracious but never loving. Stella was smart enough to understand this difference in attitude towards her, but despite her youth, she was mature enough to know that to conflict with Martin's family would have no advantage. In fact, she knew by playing the part of a welcome daughter-in-law she would gain much more. She would keep her family intact and please Martin as well.

During Martin's stay in the hospital--the first time he was away from Stella for an extended period in the seven year marriage--he had the opportunity to think about himself and his life. He began to daydream about the possibilities of escaping, somehow. He loved Stella and the children, and he didn't want to hurt them in any way. His life as a 'boy mechanic' did not fit his plan or his hopes. As a young boy, he had dreamt of being a professional. He thought about Joseph and Janette's husband - both men were educated and had positions of status in the business world.

They wore suits and ties and came home with clean fingernails. It almost made him cry to think how he was at the beck and call of Morton, who was a tyrant and a bitter man. He knew that Stella was

50

appreciative of what Mr. D had done for them - provided them with a home and giving Martin a job. But Martin had disdain for these handouts. He was not comfortable living in such proximity and dependence upon Stella's family. He had adored Claire, a sweet, loving woman, who had never been unkind to him. Mr. D. was another thing. Martin could never call him Pop. He avoided calling him anything. When he did, it was always Mr. D. *Why? Why?* he asked himself as he ran his hand through his mop of curly brown hair, sat up, and rested his head in his hands in angry despair. *If I could only find the magic solution to this problem.*

He ticked off his options and fantasized about getting away from Stella and the children - and knew he didn't have the will or really the desire to leave. Maybe Stella and the family could move to another city and find work elsewhere. Even as a mechanic, he knew that given the chance, he could someday own a business and stop coming home dirty. His dreaming stopped without any decision. He was angry and frustrated. *Maybe I'll never walk. Maybe I'll be handicapped.* These thoughts danced through his head and he shouted out loud, "Oh, hell, what's the use? I'm stuck." Pleading as if to an unknown force, "Please, someone help me!"

/ / / / / / / / / / / / / / /

Chapter Fourteen
A Young Mother

Stella was so preoccupied with the maintenance of the home, the two children, concern for her father, and Martin's health, that she often felt overwhelmed. Betty was growing up to be a bright attractive child who was intrigued by the presence of another child in the home, but still needed Stella's attention.

Betty came home from school full of wonderment and delight at the new things she was learning. Stella felt that it was becoming apparent that this child had a great capacity for learning and was full of questions, which Stella often found difficult to answer.

"Mommy, why is the sky blue, why can you only see the stars at night. Why don't I have that funny thing that the baby has between his legs? Why does Doggie have four legs and we only have two?"

Betty was studious and enjoyed reading and playing with her friends. Stella was grateful for Betty and loved her dearly. There were many problems which she faced and some of them without recourse.

Her brother, Ernst, was not very helpful and since Claire had died she didn't have another female friend in whom she could confide. She was surrounded by men and had very little interaction with them, except, Martin and Morton. Morton was becoming a bit of a concern. She did not see him very often, even though he lived and worked in the same building. She began to notice that he rarely came to visit with her and the children. He seemed to finish work, change his clothes and run off somewhere. She felt that this activity was not for a beer at the local tavern, but rather involved a woman. She thought it shameful that he would see another woman, with Claire dead only a year. Yet she reasoned that he was a young fifty-two year old man, still strong and virile. One day, he came upstairs and announced that he was moving out of his apartment below, which shocked Stella.

"What are we to do, if you leave your apartment?" Stella asked.

"No, he said, I will keep the house and we'll rent the apartment."

Hesitantly she asked, "Where are you going?"

"I am moving in with Sonia Krasnow. You remember, her husband owned the dealership in Neponsit, where I bought my last car. He died a few years back. I went there a few months ago to have the car fixed and I saw her in the office and we talked. We began to enjoy our time together. I don't want you to think that I have forgotten your mother, but I am not getting any younger, and I need a woman in my life."

With downcast eyes, unable to face him for revealing such personal thoughts, she mumbled, "I understand. Are you getting married?

He hesitated, "Not now, maybe later."

Stella felt this was certainly in character. He was crafty enough to realize that he could control the finances better, involved in a new relationship, if he were unmarried. In addition, she had her own income and probably did not want to share it with Morton.

So, Sonia became, in the parlance of the time, his common-law wife. Stella did not like this woman. She was brassy and possessive and so different from the elegant Claire. Morton noticed this coldness between the two women, but did nothing to reduce the tension. He would go about his work and drifted further apart from Stella and her family.

After advertising the available apartment, a young couple rented it. The Mahoney's were a lifesaver for Stella and Betty. Anna, the young wife of two years was going to stay in the office downstairs and help Morton with the paper-work, while John, her husband, would be another driver for the trucks which Morton seemed to collect. This arrangement was satisfactory to everyone in the two households. Anna also was a convenient baby-sitter for Betty and the baby. Anna relied on Stella for advice, even though they were almost the same age; Stella had already been married seven years and had two children.

This change of Morton leaving and the Mahoney's taking the apartment on the first floor, took place while Martin was recuperating in the hospital and Anna stayed with Betty when Stella went to visit Martin. Betty was pained every time Stella said she was going to see her Daddy. She was jealous and angry despite Stella's explanation that children were not permitted in the hospital.

On this particular Wednesday, Stella took a taxi to the Long Island Railroad in Brooklyn, Atlantic Avenue station, where she caught the train into Manhattan. She became very thoughtful about her life. Would Martin be able, physically, to continue to work as a mechanic? Would Papa find something else for him to do? What could he do, now that he had a bad leg? She was frightened and unaware that a broken leg heals and that it was not a permanent disability. It was 1925 and the unemployment was high. Although, Stella was not aware of the economics, and the post war bubble had not burst yet, she knew that there were not many opportunities for work for a man with few visible skills.

In 1925, few married woman worked. In fact, the thought never crossed Stella's mind. She had no concept of work as an option for her. In later years, this idea of her working became a horrible shock to her. In addition, she did not have a diploma from high school and she knew she would never work in a factory, as that was not in her view an activity compatible with her middle class background. She sighed and looked out the window of the train, hoping that some magician would appear and solve all of her problems. She was twenty-four years old, with the burdens of a much older person. She tried to keep herself on an even keel, but sometimes, found herself crying and wishing for a different life. She then thought of her two wonderful and beautiful children and remonstrated with herself for being so selfish. *Things will work out* she said silently, and composed herself for the visit with Martin.

/ / / / / / / / / / / / / /

Chapter Fifteen

The Entrepreneur

A few nights before Stella's visit, Joe and Evelyn had come to visit Martin. They seemed in a very good humor and laughed and joked with Martin about his 'gimpy leg'. Martin was very comfortable with his sister. He always thought she was such a beauty, and, in fact, he remarked that little Betty favored her very much. Martin also had good news. Dr. Albee had said that the leg was healing nicely and after some weeks on crutches and then a cane, he would be able to have full use of his leg. He was now confined to a wheelchair.

After they exchanged some niceties about their children, Lucille and Henry, Joe became very serious and asked, "What are your plans when you leave the hospital? Will Mr. D support you while you convalescence?"

"Yes," said Martin. "He reassured me that we would be taken care of until I was able to go back to work."

"Well, if that is what you want, it's all right with us. However, I have a proposition for you, which I want you to think about. I don't want a decision now."

Martin sat up brightly in the wheelchair and sensing that something important was going to be said, he suggested they go out to the solarium where they could talk more privately.

Joe then said bluntly, "I want you to come and work for me."

"What?" Martin asked amazed. "You don't have any trucks or machinery that needs maintenance. What could I do for you?"

"Be patient, I will explain. Never, would I offer you, my wife's brother, a job as a mechanic. No, I have more ambitious plans than that."

Martin's head began to twirl with fantasy. *Maybe, oh, maybe I can get away from dirty fingernails. Maybe I'll be able to wear a tie and a suit. Maybe, oh maybe, Stella and the family can get away from Mr. D and all his rottenness.* He knew that Joe was heavily involved with the production of chemicals. He also knew that Joe was connected with financiers who provided the capital for his chemical company. What he didn't know was that these money lenders were less than savory in many of their business dealings. And, that Joe was indebted to them for loans at usurious rates. He was soon to learn the brutal facts of Joe's enterprises and the almost Machiavellian nature of this entrepreneur's character.

Joe had grown up in lower Manhattan, on the East Side to where many immigrant families gravitated. He was the oldest of four children. He was small of stature and had a narrow long face, with small eyes squinting behind wire rimmed glasses, which he had worn since he was a young child. His mother blamed his continual reading as the cause of his bad eyes. He was thin and reedy and had little interest in befriending the boys in the neighborhood. He didn't play any of the street games which occupied so much of the time of the kids in the street. *Stoop ball, immies, ringalevio, johnny on the pony*--these games appeared infantile to him. His time was occupied with more important things.

As a young boy of thirteen or fourteen, he had already determined that he would get out of the poverty and the ghetto. He always said to himself, *It is not for me. I am Joseph Danzig and I shall make that name famous someday.* He would rush home from school to run errands for a local sweatshop manufacturing white collars, which were very popular at that time. He would get coffee and tea for the women operators or cigars for some of the bosses. He would also carry packages of completed collars to another secluded shop where lace edging or rickrack was added. All of these activities were conducted illegally. They provided work for the immigrants at a reduced rate of pay and often worked the women ten hours a day, with no provision for 'overtime' or adequate breaks in the day for relief. Joe was not bothered by the obvious exploitation of these young women. He was much more interested in the role that the bosses played. They sat at large roll-top desks, rolling cigars round and round in their mouths. They raised their voices so that they could be heard over the din of the clacking sewing machines. Their voices then were crude and raucous. The women were fair game for their jokes and abuse. Joe saw none of this. All he saw was that the owners earned more money and lived better than the workers. He was determined to follow that model. He worked several hours each day and then ran home to have dinner with his family. This was his concession to family. He did not spend much time with his family's parents or his two sisters and a brother. He found them not very interesting and certainly not people with whom he could share his plan for his future. After he helped with whatever chore was assigned to him he went into the small bedroom that he shared with his brother Adam. He'd crawl into a corner under very poor light and pore over his books, especially those related to chemistry which was his favorite school subject. He worked very hard and was an excellent student. His only purpose was to succeed. He knew that education was the key, and he planned to get as much as he could. He hated the poverty, the squalor of the tenements and kept repeating to himself his desperate need to escape the misery he saw all around him. He knew that he was smart and that given the chance, he could easily beat the system, which he saw swallowing most of the people in it. His family teased him constantly.

"Hey Joe, did you make your first million yet," his father would taunt him.

"Oh, leave me alone. I'm not bothering you, and I notice that you take the money I bring home, so leave me alone."

These teasings irritated Joseph so that dinner time was not pleasant for him and he made short shrift of the meal and left to read in his room. His siblings, decent kids, but easily influenced by their father, who was a bright man worn down by the endless struggle to stay alive. Joe's mother was so preoccupied with providing food and maintaining a semblance of family, that she seemed almost noncommittal as regards Joe. She boasted of Joe's academic prowess, but was more concerned that his small stature and less than attractive face and physique would mitigate against his ever finding a girl to marry. His mother, as were many women in her station, always looking for the answer to poverty via marriage, even though it certainly hadn't worked for many of the protagonists of this concept. But Joe was not concerned with such superficiality as looks nor did he have any natural interest. In flirting with the girls he saw in school and in the streets, he knew that someday, he would find a person who thought that intelligence, ambition, and success were more important than appearances.

And he was right—as time would show.

/ / / / / / / / / / / / / / /

Chapter Sixteen
A Future Path

For the several remaining days of Martin's stay in the hospital, he tossed around the idea that Joe had mentioned. He knew that this might be the only opportunity he would have to break from the Danvers' hold on him. He didn't' know how Stella would react. She had seemed close to her Mother, but with Claire dead and Morton off with another woman, he thought she might listen to this proposal. When Stella walked into the room the next day, her usual Wednesday visit, he greeted her so warmly, hugged and kissed her, that Stella was a little surprised. She held out a bag of hard candies that he loved.

"Thanks, but there is some real news I have to tell you. First, look how I can walk on these crutches," Martin babbled enthusiastically.

He performed for her and she looked so admiringly at this beautiful boy whom she loved so dearly and wondered what all the gaiety was about.

"If I can manage the crutches now, it won't be long before I'll be able to use a cane. Getting up the stairs will be a little problem, but I think I can manage." He stood next to her and whispered, "Let's go into the sunroom. I want to talk to you."

Stella bit her lip and worried that this would be bad news, because Martin seldom talked to her in that tone of voice.

"OK, let's go, but be careful," Stella admonished.

He ambled stiffly, down the hall, greeting patients and nurses.

He was most affable and was a genuinely happy person. He was so glad to be free of the bed and its restrictions. He was not unhappy with Stella and the children. He loved them all, but something was gnawing at him and until Joe had come with his proposal, he didn't know what it was. But now he knew! He then began to relate the details.

"Stellie, Joe and Ev were here last night and Joe offered me a job. I don't know yet what it is, but it is not as a mechanic or a truck driver, but a job with a suit," Martin exclaimed.

Stella was wide-eyed and said nothing for a few seconds to gather her composure and thoughts. She was pleased that it wasn't bad news, but was confused as to what this offer meant. She was fond of Evie, but did not like Joe for his harshness and lording over everyone in his presence.

"How and where are we going to live? What will Poppa say? What about the house?"

The words rushed out so fast that Martin grabbed her hands and said, "Whoa, we haven't decided yet. I don't know any of the details. Let's just decide that we want to make a change, a change for the better for all of us. How do you feel about it? It is important that you know." He looked at her directly. "This is probably my only chance to get the oil and dirt out from under my nails."

Tears almost filled her eyes as she said, "Was the work so bad?"

"Yes, it was bad. I had to do it considering the circumstances, but I hated it every day I worked. I love you and the kids, but I am none too pleased with Pop."

"OK, let's say yes to Joe and then we can tell Papa," Stella quickly responded.

"Oh, Stellie, I am so glad you agree. I wish I could pick you up and jump around, but thank you, thank you. You'll see this will be the beginning of a new life for all of us. I know it," Martin hugged and kissed her warmly.

Stella could see his joy and yet she was a little sad. She sensed that this was a step away from her family and a big step towards the Danzigs and the Wetzlers. She felt as if a veil had dropped down between them, a thin, but evident barrier. She feared this separation and was apprehensive and insecure. Her thoughts were wrapped up in mixed emotions – love for Martin and his happiness and yet the unease that the ties to his family would cause. One thing was sure, her life would never be the same again.

Martin returned home to convalesce, and although he was confined to the apartment, he was happy to be home with Stella and the children. What made him particularly happy was the prospect of never having to go down to the garage again and be at the beck and call of anyone who had a problem with the trucks or cars. He was anticipating the telephone call from Joseph that would change his life. He wanted so much more. He wanted to explore new faces, new places. He was ambitious and eager to translate his energy into useful and rewarding work. He was not afraid of work, but he wanted more than the drudgery of physical labor. He had total respect for those who chose to live their lives in that fashion, but not for himself.

Despite his early confrontation with poverty, his vistas were wider. He saw how the Danvers' lived and knew that set free he could have that as well. The American Dream was the brass ring to him now. He knew that given the right circumstances he could be a rich man someday. It was that work that seemed to motivate him and his entire being began to sense the glow of accomplishment which would be his someday. Money, that was what would give him the means to really enjoy life. Money, that would buy for him the clothes, the cars, and the experiences he so desperately wanted. In these dreams, Stella and the children were a part and a major part, but, and this bothered him, he even felt that his search for success was more important than wife and family.

"Martin, come here," Stella called.

Stella had pulled him out of his reverie to deal with some daily activity. Inwardly, he resented her interruption, but knew he had to come back from dreaming to reality.

"I'll be there just as soon as I manage these crutches."

He had become quite adept at crutch-walking and hoped to discard them in a few weeks when he had to return to Dr. Albee to have the heavy cast removed. It had been placed on his leg soon after surgery and was x-rayed periodically to check the degree of closure of the break. Stella wanted Martin to play with Henry, because she had to go to school to pick up Betty as they were going 'girl shopping'.

Betty was waiting for Stella at the gate in front of the school. She was a bouncy young girl, very animated about school and friends. She talked and talked. Stellie loved this child, maybe more so because of the circumstances of her conception and birth. She romanticized the incident of her birth and marveled at this child who was hers. She was determined to give her every chance to be what she wanted and that nothing would stand in her way. She sensed the change in Martin since his meeting with Joseph and Evie and knew that his ambition would be the main driving force of their life together. She knew even at that time and at her age that women would have a difficult time in the world. She thought about her Henry and knew that he would grow up in a man's world and that was half the battle. So their time together was important. Betty and Stella tried to do a lot of things together. Stella was not much good in answering all of Betty's questions but she tried to expose the child to whatever she could. Living in the small seaside town, there were not many opportunities for cultural events, if Stella was even aware of them. But, she did take Betty to the library and even to the circus when it came to town. But today they were going shopping.

School had just started. It was September, Henry was already nine months old and easier to manage, so she could leave him with the nice people downstairs or now that Martin was home convalescing, he was able to take care of Henry. Stella loved to go to the stores with Betty. They would walk down to the main street and take the trolley into Edgemere or Far Rockaway, which were larger and more affluent towns, with shops all along the street. Their plan was to go to the ice cream parlor first, where they both would indulge in ice cream sodas or sundaes.

These ice cream parlors were social gathering places. The gleaming white-tiled floors with little black diamond tiles in each corner were traditional as were the chairs and tables, which had thin wire backs and uncomfortable round cardboard seats. The tables were marble-topped. The back of the shop had a brown divider with painted glass which separated one side of the store from the other. In front, there was the fountain counter with cushioned stools and metal footrests. Betty loved to sit on the stools because they rotated and all the teenagers would sit there. She was so envious of their age and size; she just couldn't wait to grow up. Of course, the first thing one did was to go to the candy display. These, especially the chocolates, were in a showcase with a large round front and sliding doors behind. These were the expensive candies. The cheaper penny candies were displayed on a shelf in open jars and the color and enchantment of choosing made Betty so excited. She liked the licorice strings and the strips of colored dots on paper. This was not the time for concern over sugar and tooth decay. You just bought what you liked and ate.

"Oh, Mommy, these are so good."

"Keep them for after dinner," Stella admonished. "Let's have our soda and go to the stores to buy you a few new things."

After some soul searching as to the costs involved, Betty came away with a jumper or guimpe, as it was called, a few blouses, a pair of oxfords (tied shoes), stockings, and pajamas. Betty was already revealing her independence by her selection, as continued in later years, even though Stella always accompanied her shopping!

"Stella, Stella," Martin shouted as soon as he heard them come into the house. "Joseph called. I begin work just as soon as I get this cast off my leg. He says we could begin to look for a place to stay in Brooklyn, somewhere near the Danzig's."

Stella caught her breath and was so shocked by the news that she could barely talk. "Tell me all about it," she said, too calmly.

"Well, he said he would train me to be a salesman at first and

66

then teach me about the inside workings of the business so that I could then help him."

"What business is he talking about?" Stella asked.

"Oh, he has several choices for me. Honey, aren't you absolutely excited. Imagine, we can leave this little town and go back to Brooklyn away from the water and sand and find a beautiful place for all of us."

Stella was not so sure that all this excitement and anticipation about leaving the Beach would be so happy for herself. She wanted a good life for them, but to leave this place and the connection with Ernst and her friends was sad. Although her brother was a very self-sufficient young man, and wanted to be on his own, he was still in his early twenties and dependent upon Papa for support. He was really a great help to Morton. He knew the business well and was anxious and able to run it himself. Of course, Morton had no intention of relinquishing his control over the company. However, he was delighted that Ernst took such an interest in it. Stella tried to delay any dramatic change in the lives of the children and Martin agreed that they would consider a move within a year, giving them time to find a suitable home.

In the meantime, Stella tried to begin to prepare Betty for the change. She took her on a trip into Brooklyn and Fulton Street to see the department stores Namm's and Loesers. The area was beginning to become a center for commerce and industry with the nearby station of the Long Island Railroad, the Brooklyn Academy of Music, the Majestic Theatre, the Paramount, and other points of interest nearby. Betty began to appreciate that Brooklyn had much to offer. They visited the Brooklyn Museum, the Botanic Gardens and marveled at the wide streets on Eastern Parkway with many luxurious brownstone homes. Even Stella was beginning to savor the possibilities of living in a larger city not limited by the small town quality of the Beach.

Meantime, Martin was recovering his agility with the crutches and he soon was able to discard the encumbrance of the crutches and began the use of a cane. He could now manage to go down the stairs once daily and spend some time with the men in the garage. He began to feel a sense of superiority, knowing that very soon, he could appear in a suit and tie and clean hands and show the other grease-monkeys that he was now a businessman!

On a visit to Dr. Albee to have the cast removed and replaced with merely a bandage to secure the leg, he called Joseph and was invited up to his office in Manhattan. The National Chemical Corporation was located far on the West side of Manhattan down near Spring Street and was housed in a narrow building, which to Martin loomed large and foreboding. He was anxious and nervous about the impending interview and conversation with Joseph. He took the rather large elevator with the accordion metal grated door to the third floor.

He said nervously, "May I see Mr. J. Danzig? My name is Larkin."

"Oh, yes, Mr. Larkin, we have been expecting you. Just go through the glass door on the right and you will see Mr. D's office."

He limped slowly through to a corridor with a series of doors. Some were open, but down towards the end of the long hall, he saw a closed door, imprinted with, gold raised letters which said, Joseph P. Danzig, President. He was impressed and slightly intimidated.

He took a deep breath, knocked on the door and a gruff voice said, "Come in. The door is open."

Joe jumped out of his seat behind a large brown desk and pumped Martin's hand vigorously and in seeming good humor said, "Welcome, welcome, I am so glad that you are on your feet again. Here, do sit down."

Martin sheepishly chose an armchair facing the desk, but Joe said, "No, sit here," and ushered him to a softer more comfortable leather chair. Joseph took a chair and pulled it up close to Martin. In a tone of confidentiality, he murmured, "Now you are here, and we can begin!"

While Joseph went to answer a telephone call, Martin looked around the room almost surreptitiously, and noted the fine furniture, the framed pictures on the walls and family pictures on the desk and the large carved wooden humidor for cigars on the desk. He was staring at the humidor in deep thought when Joseph went to the box and offered Martin a cigar. He was astonished at the number of cigars neatly arranged in the box, with a second layer below. He loved to smoke cigars, but everyone always laughed at him, considering it very pushy looking. Smoking cigars was considered an affectation, but now, it seemed natural to him to take the cigar, bite off the end and light up. He swirled the smoke into his puffed out cheeks, and felt so wonderful at this simple event.

"All right, boy, let's get to work." He asked Martin to come to the desk and look at some papers.

Joseph came just about up to Martin's shoulder creating a notable difference in physical appearance between the two men who were contemporaries even though Joseph was about five years older. Martin was dark-haired, dark eyed, had a short straight nose and a bright slightly tanned complexion, and tended to be heavier than his frame warranted, due to his physical inactivity the past month. Joseph was short, bespectacled, blond, with a not so handsome face, had large ears that stood out, a large nose, and displayed a slightly sneering smile creasing his very thin lips. In years to come, they were called Mutt and Jeff based on the comic strip characters in the Hearst newspaper, *The Journal*, which at that time was the newspaper the Larkins read.

"This is how we are going to work it," Joe said. "When you are ready to come to work, as soon as you can, you will come into this office every day for a month so that you can learn what we do and then we will assign you to a special task, which might take you outside the building or even on a tripl. How long do you think you will have to stay home to recover?"

"As soon as I feel comfortable riding the train, I could come into the office and sit there instead of at home. I can't walk for long periods of time."

"Very good, let's say that within two weeks you come in and we will see how it goes."

Martin thanked him over and over again.

Joe said, "That's not necessary. You are going to earn your money. We need you, understand that," and gave Martin a sneering smile and wished him well.

Martin felt euphoric. He couldn't wait until he shared the news with Stella. What was peculiar about the visit was that they never spoke of one another's family. No questions were asked and no information was offered. Really strange, Martin thought, but decided to keep this aspect of the conversation to himself. He was disturbed by it, but thought that maybe that is the way that business should be conducted, even between relatives. He limped towards the train in as jaunty a manner as his cane and bad knee permitted. He blew rings of smoke, held his head up high, looked at the sky barely visible between the canyon of grey buildings and said aloud to no one in particular,

"Thank you, World, maybe now we can begin to live."

He had not a glimmer of understanding as to what Joseph did in that Chemical Company. Did he manufacture chemicals? What kind? And what would he do to promote the business?

/ / / / / / / / / / / / / / /

Chapter Seventeen

The World of Business

Joseph earned a degree in Chemistry from City College, and afterward, he went to work for a small soap manufacturer in Brooklyn, assisting in the development of soaps for different purposes. He enjoyed the challenge, but he spent more time talking to the boss about the management of the company than the boss was willing to tolerate.

"You were hired to work in the shop not in the front office," the boss would bellow. "So stay there and do your work."

Joseph saved his money and still listened carefully to the methods of the entrepreneurs in securing funds to start up a business. He visited the banks and the lending institutions and learned as much as he could about starting a business. During one of these peregrinations into the world of finance, he met two men, who were to remain his mentors, factors and delineators of the path of his business life. These two men, Roger Scharler, and Jim Scully were older, well established and wealthy bankers. They soon recognized that this young chemist was itching to spread his wings, and it didn't seem to matter which way the wind would take him. He was just anxious to fly.

They soon agreed that if Joseph was willing to take a risk, they would bankroll his starting a chemical company. He soon left the soap company and established the National Chemical Company in lower Manhattan. Scully and Scharler were the two silent but moneyed partners in this enterprise. There was much turmoil in the countries in Central America. Each of the small nations was trying to establish its hegemony and ethnic individuality. Through S&S (Scully and Scharler) and their banking connections, it was soon apparent that the manufacture of military chemicals would be a lucrative enterprise. Joseph was politically neutral at this point and did not harbor any misgivings at all in planning to manufacture Tritoluene, also known as TNT, and sell it to the highest bidder. If lives were lost as a result of his business, it was no concern of his. It did not matter either which side would require his product. His only concern was would there be a profit. As the family was not aware of the substances which were being manufactured, it was easy for Joseph to keep all interested parties unaware of the actual work at the factory. To add to the duplicitous nature of the work, he had arranged some illegal purchase of sugar from Cuba via Canada for the manufacture of a food additive product which was the ostensible purpose of the plant. To the world at large, the large vats and barrels which rolled out of the building daily were all heading for canning companies throughout the US. In fact only one tenth of the product was food and nine tenths was for clandestine military purposes for shipment to any country in Central and South America which paid for the privilege.

As can be imagined, this became a very valuable piece of property for S&S as well as an inordinate amount of profit for all parties concerned. As this was before World War II, there was no income tax and very little oversight of corporations. It was the heyday of Prohibition, and wild escapades into the world of illegalities on the part of corporations went unchecked and profits soared. It was into this milieu that Martin, the young innocent, was drawn.

/ / / / / / / / / / / / / / /

Chapter Eighteen
Martin vs. Morey

In a few weeks, Martin was able to get around more easily and felt it was time to break the news to Papa and head for the Valhalla of his dreams. He went to the garage and tried to get Mr. D's attention, and tired of waiting for him, went out to the truck yard. He started chatting with the workers who were reloading a truck, placing the orders in the proper sequence of delivery of the fresh fruit and vegetables they had picked up from the Wallabout Market, earlier in the day. He soon saw Mr. D approach. With Morton's drooping mustache, he always looked angry. Even when he was smiling, he looked angry.

Martin stood leaning on his cane and clenching his fists and his teeth, grinning inwardly, gloating at the prospect of telling his boss to go to hell with his job. He caught himself, bit his lip and remembered that he was Stella's Pop and had to be as polite as he could.

"Well, I see you are back on your feet again. Well, how soon do think you can come back to work and earn your keep," Mr. D smirked his comment.

A smile crept over Martin's face as he relished this moment of victory. "Well, er…Pop, I don't think, I'll be coming back at all."

"What are you talking about? Do you think you can be an invalid forever and that I am going to support your family while you laze away your time dreaming of God knows what?" Morton screeched. "Say what you will, but you are a grown man with a wife and family, and it is your responsibility, not mine. I'm an old man and I need to spend my remaining days in peace and not concerned with you and your ways."

"Just what do you mean by my ways?" Martin angrily replied.

"Oh, for God's sake, do I have to spell it out?" Mr. D continued, "You took an innocent young girl, made her pregnant before she had the time to grow up."

"Oh, so you think Stella was an 'innocent'?" Martin shouted in anger. "As long as we are talking, let me tell you something. I am not denying my part in this mess, but Stella came to me. I didn't go to her. It was really her idea and, well, I loved her, and, things just happened. That is not the issue here," Martin added, a bit more quietly.

"Well, what is it? I'm busy and can't stay here talking to you."

"I'll make it very short. I am not coming back to work for you. I have another job and soon we will be moving back to Brooklyn," Martin said.

"What? Where did you get a job? I know nothing about it, Are you going to work for my competition, the Levin Brothers? Is that what you call respect?" Morton was now ranting, his face flushed with anger.

"Whoa, what's the sense of talking to you? You never listen; you never care about other people. You are a selfish man whose only interest is himself," Martin countered, but now sounding mature and in control.

"So you call me selfish, and what do you think you are?" Mr. D screamed.

Martin realized there was no point in continuing this discussion and finally said, "I'm going to work for Joseph as a salesman."

"Well, I pity your wife and children; you will never amount to anything. Good riddance."

Martin was hurt and angry at this final outburst, but he contained himself and limped away. He had to be by himself for a while before he could face Stella again. Although she did not have a great love for her father, she was still living in his house and was beholden to him for her support. Maybe now they could all live peacefully again.

Martin soon discarded the cane and went to buy a new blue suit. He had gained some weight during his convalescence and Stella and he agreed that starting a new job required a new blue suit.

On a sunny Monday morning in October, he hugged the children, gave Stella a warm goodbye kiss and went off to fight the dragons in the world of business.

/ / / / / / / / / / / / / / /

Chapter Nineteen

More Thoughts

Stella had developed a routine, now that Betty was in school and Henry was in his room, happily playing with his toys. She was in the kitchen, clearing the breakfast dishes. She was thinking how happy Martin looked as he left for his work with Joseph. Even though she still had misgivings about this change, she was so happy to see Martin happy. The phone rang insistently.

"Yes, this is Stella. Who is this?"

"It's Evelyn."

"Which Evelyn?"

"Silly girl, your sister-in-law, Joe's wife."

"Oh." And then Stella breathed deeply and was silent.

Evie said, "How are you and the children?"

Stella was surprised at the call. It was the first time since she'd become a so called part of the family, nine years ago, that Evie had called to speak to her and not to Martin.

"Martin is at work, Evie."

"I know. I'm not calling to speak to him. I want to speak to you."

"Yeah, what about?" Stella almost sassily replied.

"Well, Martin tells me that you are planning to move back to Brooklyn and I wondered if you wanted me to help you find a place to live. He thought it would be nice if we lived near to one another."

"He never mentioned that to me," Stella said a bit miffed.

"Well, what do you want to do?" Evie remarked.

"Martin and I haven't talked about it much lately. He doesn't seem to have much time anymore," said Stella.

"Well yes, he has to spend more time at work and the travel is difficult. That is why it is really important that you move to Brooklyn, so that travel to the office would be easier."

A long silence followed.

"Stellie, can you get someone to watch your kids and come into Brooklyn so that we can look around?"

Reluctantly, Stella knew that the time had come to deal with this problem and she decided to agree as she knew it would make Martin happy.

"OK, I'll let you know when I can get someone to stay with Henry and get Betty home from school."

"I understand that Betty is a very smart young lady. She's eight years old and in fourth grade."

"No, she skipped a grade and is in fifth grade now," Stella proudly retorted. "I'm sorry Evie, I have to go now. I'll call you tomorrow."

After a few days of discussion with the family downstairs, Martin and Stella finally decided that Stella and Evie would meet at Evie's Brooklyn home and they would venture into the 'apartment looking mode'. This was a new experience for Stella as she never had to face this task independently. She had lived at home and then, when married, at her parent's home.

Martin met them at Evie's and they went to Ocean Parkway, a beautiful tree lined street, with large homes facing a central bridle path and walkway with benches for families, children and neighborly talk.

Here and there were a few small six story apartment buildings. They seemed out of place among the sprawling brick homes. Stella was disappointed when they began to look at the apartment buildings. She didn't understand how so many families could crowd into one building. They finally decided on a first floor two bedroom apartment, which faced both Ocean Parkway and Avenue C. It was a light airy place, very convenient to food markets and other neighborhood stores. The schools were fairly close, but at the moment, Stella was more concerned with the move itself. Martin and Stella signed the lease, and they decided to move within the month.

Martin was so happy, as was Evie. Stella was tolerant of the excitement, but really didn't share it. She felt as if life was being decided for her and that she had little to say. She knew that now the sphere of interest would shift and Martin would now be in the 'bosom' of his family and she would be the outsider. They returned to Evie's home quite a distance away, so they took the trolley which brought them a bit closer. After some continued discussion on how wonderful it will be for the children to live in such a beautiful place, with no more trucks, no more truck drivers, etc. Stella felt very hurt by this reference to her father and how he made his living. She saw nothing to be ashamed of, but Evie and Martin had other ideas.

Stella and Martin discussed how they would raise the question of moving to Betty. By this time, Betty was thoroughly involved with friends, with her new piano lessons, and her school work. Her love of learning was so apparent and her happiness with her young life as it was, pained Stella. She knew this move would be a terrible shock to the child, disrupting her routines, leaving her playmates, and the only home she remembered.

Martin decided that he would undertake the task of telling Betty. He called her Boopsie and loved her deeply. Betty was enchanted with her Daddy. He always played with her, teased her, so different from Momma, who was always telling her to do something. Betty knew that her parents loved her. They told her so always, but Daddy was different. After much hesitation, Martin and Betty had just finished dinner and he asked her what was happening in school. Classes had just started a few weeks ago.

"Well, Boopsie, how is my genius doing? Do you already know more about everything than I do?"

Betty felt giggly and responsive. "Daddy, you are so silly."

"Well, there is one thing, which I want to tell you about."

She climbed up on the leather armchair which was large enough for both Martin's ample girth and Betty.

"Betty, dear, you are a big girl and I am going to tell you something which may make you sad, so listen to the whole story first."

He then proceeded to explain that because of the accident, he could no longer work for Grandpa, as it hurt his leg too much. Uncle Joseph had given him the chance to work in the city and the work would not be difficult. He also tried to make her understand that they would have to move. Betty started to cry and worried about her piano teacher and her friends from school. He told her that they would try to have them all come and visit them in the new house in Brooklyn. Betty raised many questions of friends and school and how she would feel lonely without the things she loved.

After some petting and reasoning, Betty began to see this as an opportunity to shine among her friends and boast a bit about her new home, new friends and new experiences. Martin was satisfied that he had neutralized one member of the family. He knew that Stella was not exactly excited by the idea. He knew that she was not fond of Joseph and had her suspicions as to his motives. She was very perceptive, but kept her thoughts to herself. At this point, she didn't want to do anything to jeopardize her life and the children's future.

The task of packing and moving to a new life occupied her time and her family. Betty and Henry included, began to fit into the mode and the daily routines were only slightly interrupted by the cartons, boxes, and barrels strewn everywhere. Just as everything seemed to fall into place, Betty came home from school, complaining of a pain in her stomach. Her temperature was elevated. The doctor was called and a rush to the hospital ensued, where an emergency appendectomy was performed. Stella and Martin were very concerned, but Betty seemed the least perturbed. She felt so much better after the surgery and enjoyed all the attention this hospitalization afforded her. After a ten day stay and convalescence at home, she was well enough to return to school within a few weeks. This, however, delayed the move. Stella had almost finished the packing and, as Martin was busy at the office, this burden was hers.

Within a few weeks, the packing completed, the goodbyes made, the trek to their new home began. For the children it was an adventure, for Martin a step to the realization of his dream, to Stella, a painful change.

/ / / / / / / / / / / / / / /

81

Chapter Twenty

Brooklyn Again

Their apartment in Brooklyn was certainly adequate. The rooms were large and as it was a corner apartment, it had many windows, allowing for natural ventilation during the warmer months. The newness of the change, the development of new friends, the excitement of having her Daddy home earlier, and the visits with her cousins made Betty happy. It was true that she had to walk a greater distance to school and there were many more automobiles in the streets, as well as trolley cars on tracks in the middle of some major thoroughfares. However, school was such an integral part of her life that she soon adjusted. Betty began to write down everything that she did in a day. She soon developed the idea for a diary. She didn't want to tell Stella, because she wanted it to be her secret. So she took some old notebook paper poked two holes on the top with a pencil and tied the pages together with a ribbon.

At first, the pages merely reflected her day's activities with Awoke at 7:30, Dressed, Ate Breakfast, Went to school, etc. But soon this didn't seem to be enough and she began to write about the family and thoughts about herself and her friends. Then she began a listing of the books she read. She took graph paper and listed the year, month and day and wrote the title and author and a brief comment on her reaction to the text. Henry was getting bigger and on Saturdays, Mom and Daddy would give her a quarter and with Henry in tow, they'd walk the few blocks to the Culver Theatre, where they sat through a double feature and a serial. Betty, at first, liked the idea of being the older sister taking Henry to the movies, but after a while she resented this duty but dutiful as she was, they continued the practice year after year.   Here too, she took graph paper and recorded the movies and the stars who performed and kept meticulous notes. Betty soon graduated from PS 217 as the youngest in her class and then moved on to Montauk JHS on 18th Ave. and Henry went to PS 42.   Here again Betty had to take him to school and then rush the additional few blocks to get to her school. One day, Betty and Henry were entering Henry's school when Henry refused to go up to his classroom. Betty began pleading with him as she was fearful of getting to her class late. She was a very proper and industrious student.   However, Henry was adamant. Soon, the principal, whose office was on the same floor as Henry's class, came out into the hallway to investigate the noise.

"And what is the trouble here?" she screeched.

Henry then stated that the teacher had called him a "sissy" to be wearing a coat with a fur collar. Grandpa Larkin, who now had his own business, made a camel's hair coat with a beaver collar for Henry, which he disliked intensely. The principal then began pulling Henry, now screaming and crying, into the classroom and forced him into his seat, and insisted that he wear the coat as punishment for saying that the teacher had been involved in such an action. The principal told the teacher to hold him there as Henry began to bounce about in defiance. Betty was torn between trying to protect her brother and the need to get to her own school. The principal ran out of the room, and returned quickly with a flower vase and threw the water over Henry and said, "Now sit there in your wet clothes." Henry was so stunned that he sat there immobilized. Betty ran to her school, frightened and crying.

When they both came home and related the incident, Martin was so enraged that he went to the school the following day. Stella was concerned that Henry might have become ill as a result of sitting in wet clothes for several hours. Henry was acting strangely as well. He did not eat his food and just wanted to sleep. Martin never got to see the principal. She was out of the building at a meeting, he was told. Within a day or so, Henry began to complain of an earache. The doctor suggested hospitalization. The doctor diagnosed the infection behind Henry's left ear as an inflammation of the mastoid bone and suggested surgery to removes the diseased portion. This was called mastoiditis. This was before antibiotics came on the scene and Henry's left ear was always more flattened than the right, as a portion of the bone had been removed via the mastoidectomy.

Betty was now ten years old and she was eligible for the Special Progress classes where the seventh through ninth grades were accordioned into two years. She soon graduated from ninth grade and Martin purchased a ring to celebrate the event. As the ring had diamonds and sapphires, Stella did not approve of a twelve year old child wearing it. It remained in Stella's jewelry box until Betty, at about age forty-five, found and reclaimed it. Martin also bought a signet ring with a small chip for himself which he wore on the "pinky" of his left hand and would become his 'signature' for the rest of his life.

During these years Betty befriended a few girls and soon became aware of her developing body and her interest in boys. She was totally ignorant of her body's physiology as Stella was of the old

84

school and menstruation and sex were topics that were never discussed.

One day, Betty was playing across the street from her house and the girls and boys were climbing a fence, when one of the older girls, yelled at Betty and said, "Hey, your lady friend arrived. You'd better go take care of it."

She didn't have the vaguest idea what they were talking about, but felt something warm in her panties and ran home. In the bathroom she was shocked at the sight of the blood and in tears called to Stella. Stella then said, "Ok, bless you, you are now a woman and this will happen every month, but don't tell Daddy."

Betty didn't understand why this should be kept a secret from her Daddy as every scratch she had was dutifully reported. But she kept her promise and now her diary would reflect this important event. In the street, the wild girl, Ray, kept her properly informed and as was usual, she learned the "facts" from her friends in the street. Her mother never discussed this or anything else with her and, of course, the topic was off-limits with her father. As she got older and began to have relationships with men, she often wondered if her reactions would have been different had she been better informed.

In the meantime, their economic status improved. Martin purchased a new car; Betty's wardrobe now included well-made clothes. Her Grandpa Larkin had the workers in his shop make many attractive outfits for her. One particular outfit she loved was a coat made of pale purple velvet with a grey squirrel collar and a cloche hat to match with a pompom on the side. One Easter, Stella had a new suit and wore a brown close-fitting hat, and a string of fur pieces which were fox pelts and were attached by the mouth biting the tail of the second skin. At about this time, Aunt Minerva and Jack with Rosalie and Harriet, who were living in a small apartment in another section of Brooklyn, had moved into an apartment across the street. Harriet was just a few months older than Betty, a very pretty and sweet child, but unfortunately, she developed juvenile diabetes which dogged her all the years of her life. The Smiths were not very financially secure as Jack, Harriet's father, never made much money, but Harriet and Betty were good friends and spent time together. This particular Easter, the whole family was decked out in finery and they planned to take pictures of the occasion.

Martin said, "Let's get to it. Where is Henry?"

Henry wore a white suit which set off the very handsome face he now had. He was a devilish young boy, and soon was sliding down the coal chute to see where the coal went. Needless to say, Martin and Stella roundly reprimanded the young boy and the photo did not show his beautiful suit but a replacement.

Martin and Stella began to think of purchasing a house, or at least moving into a private house where there would be a garden and better accessibility to the street. Soon, they began a search for a house. Characteristic of this community were two-family homes. They were well-built brick houses with two private entrances, a garage and long driveways that led to a yard. They were two-family homes with shade trees and grassy garden plots in front and back. The family moved and great fanfare ensued. All the families, the Smiths, Wetzlars, and Danzigs greeted the move with joyful expressions of good wishes and small gifts. Evelyn helped Stella secure the services of a decorator, and heavy drapes were installed on the windows with braided rope tie-backs. An oriental Sarouk rug was on the living room and dining room floors. With the two children in school, and Martin at work, Stella felt that the American dream had come true. She was happy, but always there was the undercurrent of anxiety, that all of this would not last.

During this period of affluence for Martin and his family, Joseph was accumulating profits at a rapid rate. He was determined to be successful and he chose to keep the information as to the main source of his wealth confined to his inner circle of financial barons. He did not share his nefarious schemes with those whom he did not trust and very few fit that bill. The visible and legal activity in the company was still the development of chemical additives for food preservation and certain agricultural products. These products were sold through the work of Martin and a few other salesmen. Martin had developed this skill and was able to sell the product effectively. He was a very charismatic man who was able to engage the customers and secure orders. He was totally unaware that the majority of the workers in the factory were manufacturing chemicals, which, although basically the same agricultural formulae were indeed also the basis for the production of TNT. This material was then sold to any willing client.

At this period in time, most of the clients were participants in what was euphemistically called the Border Wars of the "Banana Republics" in Central and South America. All the arrangements were developed and monitored by Scharlin and Co., the wealthy financial backers of Joseph's enterprises. A separate corporation existed on paper and there were only three members, Danzig, Scharlin, and Scully. A separate set of books delineating the sales and receipts were kept in a safe away from the plant. It was a remarkable feat of double-faced dealings at which Joseph had become a master. His concept of integrity was confined to his estimation of the difference between good and evil. To him, there was only one criterion for determination of the difference between good and bad, to him as simple as black and white. The question was: *Would the bottom line reflect a reasonable profit?* One would imagine that with the illegal activities, that he would fear the consequences of exposure. However, he did not. He thought he was invincible.

In order to maintain the image of a good husband and father, he decided to expand his holdings in a more visible way. One summer, the Wetzlars and Danzigs visited a resort in Rockland County and enjoyed the location and its proximity to NYC. New City was a growing resort with small cottages dotting the rural landscape. Joe soon began to inquire as to the availability of land and eventually purchased thirty acres of wooded land at the top of a small rise called Red Hill Road. He magnanimously gave some of the acreage to Grandpa and sold some of it to the Wetzlars. All three built summer homes. Janine Wetzlar and Evelyn Danzig, Martin's sisters, chose to share a common driveway at the top of the hill and this driveway was planted with birches which, over the years came to give the property the landmark name of "The Birches".

Grandma and Grandpa Larkin built a house around the curve in the road which was a five minute walk on the road or a three minute walk through the trees from behind the Birches.

Joseph never consulted or ever offered Martin and Stella the opportunity to share in the land purchase or to be considered for building a house. They were definitely not in the same class. Martin was only a salesman and worked for Joe. This, plus the long-standing antipathy Joe felt towards Stella, mitigated against their possible inclusion in this deal. When the homes were ready for use, the families began to spend more and more time there. Grandma and Grandpa relocated there permanently, and would become their last home. Within a few years, both families gave up their homes in Brooklyn and moved to New City.

/ / / / / / / / / / / / / / /

Chapter Twenty-one
Changes

One rainy Sunday morning, several years later, Martin and Stella were having breakfast, while the children were in their rooms doing homework when Martin abruptly put his newspaper down and faced Stella,

"Stellie, I have to talk to you about some changes."

"Like what?"

"Well, I have to go on the road to begin to open a new territory to sell our products. Now that I have the experience of selling in the NY area, over these past few years, Joe wants me to broaden our selling area."

Stella tried hard to control her anger and stiffly said, "Of course, he wants you out of the way. You know Marty; I just don't trust him."

"Stellie, why are you so hard? Why don't you accept what I tell you?"

"I don't accept it, because I know him better than you do. Watch out, Martin. Watch out!!"

Martin tried to reason with Stella, but she was adamant.

She got up from the table and busied herself at the sink as her eyes filled up with tears. They were both still under thirty and their dreams differed. Hers were for home and children; he saw glitter and rainbows over the horizon.

Soon, Martin began to travel the northeast territory. He came home every few weeks and stayed for a week and then left again. As a consequence, he became less and less involved in domestic concerns. Betty missed his attention and daily presence. Henry seemed to be unaffected. Stella tried very hard to maintain a semblance of normalcy. She never yielded to the deeper hidden feelings that something had been happening to her marriage. She kept up a facade of contentment and presented herself, Martin, and family as if all were well. Her signals to the world and family were: *Don't come too close, and don't ask any more than the cursory questions of me, like how are you?*

Often, Stella, Betty, and Henry would visit with the aunts for Sunday dinners. These really were Stella's aunts, her mother, Claire's, siblings. Lena, who had no children, seemed to invite the family most often. Betty and Henry liked these outings. For Betty, it was a chance to dress up and play with all the cousins, who were really Stella's cousins, but because Stella had been such a young mother, all the cousins were about the ages of Betty and Henry. Henry, of course, was always horsing around. It didn't seem as if there was a serious bone in his body. Here, he had a greater audience and he made full use of it.

/////////////////

Chapter Twenty-Two
Accident #3

Several years had passed and many changes had taken place in the family. Papa Danvers, Stella's father, had died and left all of his money to his 'wife', denying to Stella and Ernst any part of the estate. Stella was hurt and angry, and tried to understand her father's motivation. She finally accepted the reality that he was not a very generous man and that his family was never uppermost in his mind and heart. Ernst, however, seemed to have learned from his father everything about trucking and produce. He came to Brooklyn, opened a business in Bush Terminal, met a young woman, Elise, and married. She was a bookkeeper in one of the companies with which he did business. She always appeared cold and unattractive to Stella, but they tried to maintain a reasonably good relationship. She continued to work for a few years after their marriage and then she settled into raising a family. Cora and Morton were their two children, Cora about Henry's age and Morton, younger.

Ernie and Elise were always invited to these Sunday dinners, but rarely appeared. There always was something going on among the Fortrell's (Elise's family) and Elise remained distant. Martin also was a rare presence at these events. Stella always responded with, "*He's on the road.*"

Martin continued to enjoy the fruits of his labors. He wore gold cufflinks, a pinky ring, wore expensive shirts and suits and affected stylish fedoras, which he wore jauntily tilted to one side.

Along with his new station in life, he found less time to spend at home. He looked forward to the company of his male colleagues. He was young and attractive, but he did not seek female attention at this point. Stella seemed aware of the changes in Martin, but although she sensed that he spent less time at home, he still came home and was providing for her and the children.

One Friday evening, Martin said he would be late for dinner and not to wait for him. He was using the car that day, as the thought of Stella learning to drive did not seem part of her role. At about midnight, the front door bell rang, and Stella frightened by the thought of something dreadful happening, opened the door to two police officers trying to keep Martin, obviously very drunk, on his feet.

"We found him driving erratically on Ocean Parkway," one officer related. "He hit a tree and stopped. As the vehicle was moving very slowly, neither the driver nor the vehicle suffered any damage. The car was towed to a garage and we drove him home."

Stella was quite upset but managed to get some coffee into Martin, and he slept until noon the next day. He explained that the salesmen were meeting with Joe and a few other men, and there was plenty of alcohol on the table. Things became ugly as an argument ensued and Martin left in a huff.

"Did all the men drink and become drunk as you did?" Stella inquired.

Martin, sheepishly replied, "I don't remember."

Stella had always felt that anyone who drank to an excess and looked like Martin did on that Friday night was a bum. That connotation made her very angry and resentful. This situation did not sit well with Stella. For the next few weeks, there was friction and anxiety between them. Stella watched Martin's every action and he felt constrained by these circumstances. Instead of openly discussing the problem, it festered deeper and deeper and resolution seemed very far away.

As Martin had been diagnosed with diabetes, these alcoholic binges were very unhealthy. Stella had discussed this episode with Evelyn, but she remained tight-lipped and refused to condemn either Joe or Martin. Stella soon realized that she would have to deal with the situation herself.

Joe, too, was irritated, firstly, by Martin's questioning the policy of manufacturing agricultural products, but essentially producing TNT. Secondly, there was Martin's irresponsible drinking. He was determined to fire him. Evie, Joe's wife, interfered and begged Joe to think of Stella and the children, and he relented. But all would not be the same. Martin's work life took a downward turn.

He was told to 'go on the road', which essentially made him a 'traveling salesman'. This was a downgrade which Martin resented but accepted as a fact. He was no longer considered a part of the inner circle and certainly not privy to the many company secrets, which some, he reasoned were not legal. An additional wrinkle had begun to take place, which involved Joe and the company. This meant the purchase of sugar from Cuba transshipped to Canada and then to the US to avoid certain tariffs. Martin had known this and had indicated his objection to the method of shipping to Canada. Joe had been furious with Martin at that Friday night meeting and had been intent upon firing him.

As life had become more comfortable for Stella, Martin felt constrained by these circumstances even though their financial situation had improved. The relationship with the Larkins (Martin's family) was more amenable. The children were well. All was fine, except for one problem. She began to notice that Martin was coming home later each evening proclaiming that work related meetings and dinners kept him busy. Instead of openly discussing the problem, it festered deeper and deeper and resolution seemed far away.

She accepted this reality as part of their increased financial social status. They moved into a home, the first of their own. She engaged the services of a decorator and in the fashion of the times, the living room was heavily laden with draperies and thick Turkish Sarouk carpets. There was a car in the driveway and all seemed happy and secure.

Martin continued to work with Joe, but his role in the operation seemed to have changed after the drinking episode. Martin knew this, was involved with the details, and that Friday night when all the 'generals' met, and they began to debate the use of this method of transshipment to Canada, Martin, quite vociferally objected to this method. Joe was furious and was intent on firing him as he could not tolerate any dissension from his proclaimed authority. However, Evelyn urged Joe to find another position for Martin in order to keep the family supported.

The incident that Friday evening was beginning evidence of the change in Martin's role as a salesman for Joseph. His territory was Pennsylvania and Ohio where he could find acceptance of the products dealing with agriculture and steel manufacturing. It was a lonely, dusty world. He was an easy target for alcohol abuse. He lived in hotels, made few friends, and spent his free time in bars.

He did go home several times a month. These visits were leaden. He was an outsider. He groped for an entry into their lives. Henry was young and didn't miss him. Stella began to build a wall brick by brick – of anger and resentment and loneliness, keeping Martin at a distance. The only warmth he felt and relished was from Betty. She always was happy to see him and the affection between them was unstructured and genuine. Betty loved and missed her father. The eternal question was, *"When will I see you again?"*

This period after Martin's transfer to the road and traveling was marked by Betty's high school years between 1930 and 1933. She was a good student and made friends easily. She soon was thinking about boys.

/ / / / / / / / / / / / / / /

Chapter Twenty-Three

Philadelphia

Martin was becoming disenchanted with the non-existent glamour of his ascendancy into the world of business. Martin quickly deteriorated into an alcoholic. He found himself sleeping off his drunken binges and working less and less. His income dropped. He found himself neglecting to call on customers and ending his workday earlier and earlier. Instead of seeing clients, he would seek out the nearest bars and spend the evening drinking. He was aware of the effect excessive drinking could have on his diabetes and tried to eat to soak up the booze. He then would go to the local hotel sit in the lobby and smoke a cigar and soon wander off to bed. Sometimes he would drop into auction houses and sit quietly and sleepily in the back rows. He was fascinated by the auctioneers' techniques as well as the role of the shills. These well-trained co-workers knew how to effectively raise the amount of money indicated by the legitimate bidders.

Joe insisted that he shape up or he was out of a job. He resisted Evelyn's pleading. Finally, Joe ditched him leaving him hanging by his fingernails in Philadelphia. Martin then began a series of letters to Stella describing his situation, pleading for understanding, and asking for money. In one of his letters, he urged her to take care of herself and the children and forget about him. Stella, in turn, moved to a smaller apartment, convinced that Martin was no longer a part of her life.

/ / / / / / / / / / / / / / /

Chapter Twenty Four

Betty and Milk

Betty and Henry were growing up and seemed quite different in personality. Betty was serious and cared about learning. Stella encouraged her at every opportunity. Henry was always mischievous. One summer, this was illustrated in a very dramatic way. On the street, just a few houses away lived a family called the Benders. Husband and wife worked together in a store they owned down near Fulton Street. They sold fabrics, buttons, and other notions, such as ribbons, elastics, etc. There were two children, a twelve-year-old girl, Francie, and a five-year-old, Bobbie. Supervising the house during the day was a black housekeeper called Ella. Henry loved little Bobbie and Bobbie in turn was fascinated and intimidated by Henry's activities.

One summer day, Henry urged Bobbie to ask Ella, the housekeeper, for some money for ice cream, and Henry came in to Stella with the same request. As the ice cream truck was expected, this was not an unusual request. Henry asked Bobbie what he would like, and Bobbie said that he would like a hot dog. The only connection that Henry had with hot dogs was when the family went to Nathan's in Coney Island.

So Henry said, "OK, Bobbie, let's go."

When dinner time came, Stella sent Betty out to get Henry. He was nowhere t be found. Ella was out looking for Bobbie as well. As darkness began to fall, the families' anxiety reached such proportions that Ella called the police. The cops looked down the large pit where the new subway was to be. They scoured the area with no success. Anxiety soon led to panic and hospitals were called. Fears and tears soon followed.

Just as the police were ready to leave and list the boys as missing, someone shouted, "Here they are. Here they are!"

Two bedraggled smudged kids holding hands straggled into view. Stella and Ella ran to gather up the boys.

Stella shouted, "Where were you? What did you do?"

"Nothing," Henry said. "We just went to Coney Island to get hot dogs for Bobbie and me."

"Coney Island?" Ella said. "That's five miles away. How did you get there?"

"Well, we took the ice cream money and went on the trolley," Henry said. "The man did not charge us. When we got to Coney Island, we bought hot dogs and then some custard, and then we didn't have any more money. We tried to get on the trolley, but the man wouldn't let us on. So we walked in the tracks and followed the trolley home. Bobbie got tired, so I carried him for a while, and then we stopped to rest."

Needless to say, there were some new rules set in place for Henry and Bobbie. Betty, at this point, was twelve and ready to graduate from junior high. Grandpa Larkin had made her graduation dress, and Martin gave her a diamond ring. Stella thought this a bit too ostentatious for a twelve-year-old, but both Betty and Martin were delighted. Betty would now enter Erasmus Hall High School, a very prestigious school, built originally by the Dutch. The Dutch Reformed Church still stood opposite the school. The old building on the grounds was the original school, and the floor boards were secured with wooden pegs. Some classes were still held there. The school had entrance archways, and the buildings extended from Flatbush to Bedford Avenues. As the buildings were on the periphery, the grassy center was called the quadrangle. Betty was delighted to attend this lovely place. She could take the trolley up Church Avenue, which stopped on the corner of Flatbush Avenue. Many times she walked home.

She was beginning to become accommodated to her way of life: school, home, library, movies. She felt happy - only if her Daddy would be home more. She and her family were soon in for a new shock. At dinner one evening, Stella announced to Betty and Henry that Daddy was not sending as much money home as in the past, and it was necessary for them to move to a less expensive place. Stella did not explain any further. It became apparent also that Martin was coming home less frequently, and when he did, he did not seem to be his own regular happy self.

The family relocated to an apartment on 51 Street. They occupied the upper floor; the Gold family, the owners, lived in the apartment below. The space was adequate, but this time Betty's room was in the front of the house and the other two bedrooms were in the back. Betty's life was predicated on study and school work, at which she excelled. She felt the pinch economically. Jobs were not readily available and Betty, like all young women, tried to help their families through the desperate, depressed period, by after school and Saturday work. Betty, younger than most, was not successful and Stella did not push her.

Betty had blossomed into a lovely young woman. She no longer had the dresses and coats that represented her expansive life when she was in junior high. There were fewer outings and time was spent at home listening to the radio, reading, and schoolwork. The few girlfriends she had were not very much better situated and the problems of the political changes that were taking place in Europe began to spill over into this country. She and the family, mostly Stella, began to read the newspapers with a different outlook. Martin was a Hearst paper enthusiast, and until his less frequent appearances, that was the reading in the house. But soon, Stella and Betty began to take an interest in the world outside. Henry was not particularly interested in this subject. He was beginning to have an awareness of girls, money, and sports. This followed him throughout his life.

Every afternoon, after school, Stella would have Betty walk two blocks away to purchase milk from a grocery. At that time, milk was kept in large milk cans and the grocer would use a dipper and fill the container his customer brought. Home delivery of milk was available at this time, but the extra cost was not in Stella's budget. Betty took a small aluminum milk can with a handle and cover and went to get the few items which Stella needed. Stella was exceedingly frugal and made good use of whatever funds she received. Between the money sent by Martin and the few dollars she squeezed out of her brother, she was able to manage.

One Thursday in late April 1932, the smell of summer in the air put a smile on Betty's face thinking that in a few months, in June would be her fifteenth birthday and although she didn't expect anything special to happen, she was happy.

Stella called to her, "Betty, we only need milk and bread for breakfast."

Betty shook off the day dreaming and answered quickly, "Okay, Mom, I'll be ready in a minute."

As Betty left the second floor of their two-family house, swinging the milk can in hand, hopping down the steps, she remarked to herself that she never felt deprived. Her only feeling of deprivation arose from the loss of her father's affection. She did miss all the lovely clothes that her Grandpa had made for her when she was in junior high, but now all of the girls were as simply dressed as she was.

As Betty passed the next street she noticed a young blond boy sitting on the steps of his house. She glanced at him and as she approached, she felt his eyes on her. He didn't move, but just stared. She lifted her chin and walked haughtily by. She bent down to tie her loosened lace and saw him still gazing at her. When she returned, she looked for him, but instead of standing on the steps, he was inside the front porch, leaning out of the window. He smiled as she passed.

As the weeks passed, she often noticed him either on the steps or peering out of his front porch window. She was intrigued, amused and wondering. Each time she passed his house, she silently checked to see whether he was there. Most times he was inside watching her as she passed. She made no visible recognition, but inwardly she was excited to think that this handsome boy could be interested in her.

Betty
AGE 15

JAN. 1	"GOOSE MAN"	S. WASSERMAN
2	K	M.R. RHINEHART.
FEB 3	"STRANGE INTERLUDE"	E. O'NEILL
MAR 4	"DORIAN GRAY"	O. WILDE
5	"JOHN GRISHAM'S DAUGHTER"	C. MERREL
PR 6	"LADY BIRD"	G. HILL
7	"THE KENWORTHYS"	M. WILSON
8	"FRUITLANDS"	J. GALSWORTHY
9	"OFFER OF MARRIAGE"	B. RUCK
10	"GRAY YOUTH"	R. ONIONS
11	"VILLAGE DOCTOR"	S. KAYE-SMITH
12	"SEPTIMUS"	W. LOCKE
13	"AMERICAN BEAUTY"	E. FERBER
14	"SPELL LAND"	S. KAYE SMITH
15	"STORM BURY"	E. PHILLPOTTS
16	"GILAND"	R.W. CHAMBERS
17	"TIN SOLDIER"	P. BAILEY
18	"TORCH SONG"	K. NORRIS
19	"DOAN'S ELBOW"	A.W. MASON
20	"MAMMON"	P.C. WREN
21	"NINA"	S. ERTZ
22	"SATURDAY'S CHILD"	K. NORRIS
23	"WHITE FAWN"	O.H. PROUTY
24	"TENDER TALONS"	H.R. MARTIN
25	"PARIS BOUND"	P. BARRY
26	"THAT'S GRATITUDE"	F. CRAVEN
27	"THEIR FATHER'S GOD"	O.E. ROLVAAG
28	"TOP OF THE WORLD"	E.M. DELL
Aug 29	"DEVIL IN THE CHEESE"	T. CUSHING
30	"MISTRESS OF HUSABY"	S. UNDSET
31	"VINEGAR TREE"	
32	"PHILLIPPA"	A. SEDGWICK
33	"ALL KNEELING"	A. PARRISH
34	"TWO SHIPS"	V. NORRIS
35	"Ripley's Believe It Or Not" 2nd Editi	R. RIPLEY
36	"THE GOOD EARTH"	P.S. BUCK
37	"DODSWORTH"	S. LEWIS
38	"UNVEILED"	B.K. SEYMOUR
39	"FALSE PURPLE"	S. HORLER

BOOKS READ IN 1932   Betty AGE - 15

40	"PERMANENT ECLIPSE"	M. MAURICE
41	"THE SPECIALIST"	C. SALE
42	"STRATHMORE"	"OUIDA"
43	"PHILIP GOES FORTH"	G. KELLEY
44	"FOUNTAIN SEALED"	A. SEDGWICK
45	"WESTWARD PASSAGE"	M. A. BARNES
46	"ROPERS ROW"	W. DEEPING
47	"LES MYSTERES DE PARIS"	E. SUE
48	"ASHENDEN"	W. S. MAUGHAM
49	"CHILDREN OF THE AGE"	K. HAMSUN
50	"WINDING LANE"	P. GIBBS
51	"DAISY MAYME"	G. KELLY
52	"LAP OF LUXURY"	B. RUCK
53	"SHORN LAMB"	W. J. LOCKE
54	"WATERS UNDER THE EARTH"	M. OSTENSO
55	"ESSAYS"	C. MORLEY
56	"UNDER DISPUTE"	A. Repillo
57	"SPOON RIVER ANTHOLOGY"	E. L. MASTERS
58	"HARNESS"	A. GIBBS
59	"CHERI"	"COLETTE"
60	"FOUR MONTHS AFOOT IN SPAIN"	R. FRANCK
61	"BELLE-MERE"	K. NORRIS
62	"READING AN ESSAY"	H. WALPOLE
63	"POEMS"	A. NOYES
64	"OLD DARK HOUSE"	J. B. PRIESTLEY
65		
66		

SHOWS - JOLLY

"BEST YEARS"   MAJESTIC
"GREEN PASTURES"   MAJESTIC

MOVIES IN 1932

40 "SO BIG" — BARBARA STANWYCK
41 "MERRILY WE GO TO HELL" — FREDRIC MARCH
42 "MOUTHPIECE" — WARREN WILLIAM
43 "COHENS AND KELLYS IN HOLLYWOOD" — George Sidney / Irene Donne
44 "SYMPHONY OF SIX MILLION" — RICHARD TALMADGE
45 "GET THAT GIRL" — EDWARD G. ROBINSON
46 "TWO SECONDS" — TOM BROWN
47 "FAST COMPANIONS" — EDNA MAY OLIVER
48 "LADIES OF THE JURY" — Paul Muni
49 "SCARFACE SHAME OF A NATION"
50 "WEEKENDS ONLY"
51 "FREAKS" — Wallace Ford
52 "JEWEL ROBBERY" — WILLIAM POWELL
53 "THE RICH ARE ALWAYS WITH US" — RUTH CHATTERTON
54 "ROADHOUSE MURDER" — Dorothy Jordan
55 "HOLLYWOOD SPEAKS"
56 "THIRTEENTH GUEST" — GINGER ROGERS
57 "RADIO PATROL" — ROBERT A. RUSSELL
58 "SHADOW BETWEEN"

59 "FIRST YEAR"
60 "HOLD 'EM JAIL"
61 "AMERICAN MADNESS" — WALTER HUSTON
62 "NIGHT WORLD" — LEW AYRES
63 "STRANGE LOVE OF MOLLY LOUVAIN" — Ann Dvorak
64 "WHAT PRICE HOLLYWOOD" — MARILYN MONROE
65 "BY WHOSE HAND" — Ben Lyon
66 "THEY NEVER COME BACK" — Regis Toomey
67 "MADAME RACKETEER" — ALISON SKIPWORTH
68 "DRIFTING SOULS"
69 "HORSE FEATHERS" — MARX BROTHERS
70 "HELL'S HIGHWAY" — RICHARD DIX
71 "BACK STREET" — CHARLES BOYER
72 "VANISHING FRONTIER"
73 "RAIN" — Walter Huston
74 "PHANTOM OF CREST WOOD" — RICARDO CORTEZ
75 "BIG AS FORD LAST"
76 "SMILIN' THROUGH" — JEANETTE McDONALD / en Français
77 "HEART PUNCH"
78 "TESS OF THE STORM COUNTRY" — MARY PICKFORD
79 "THAT'S MY BOY" — MARTIN LEWIS ✓✓

105

79 Movies Went to in 1932

JAN 1	"LADIES OF THE BIG HOUSE"	
FEB 2	"GIRLS ABOUT TOWN"	Kay Francis
3	"UNHOLY GARDEN"	Ronald Coleman
4	"ALEXANDER HAMILTON"	George Arliss
5	"PRIVATE LIVES"	Norma Shearer
6	"SPORTING CHANCE"	Kristen Stewart
7	"HIS WOMAN"	N/A
MAR 8	"THE DELEWER"	Lloyd Hughes
9	"TABU"	Ann Chevalier
10	"NECK AND NECK"	Walter Huston
11	"MAKER OF MEN"	N/A
12	"NIGHT BEAT"	
13	"MATA HARI"	Greta Garbo
14	"UNDER EIGHTEEN"	N/A
15	"UNEXPECTED FATHER"	Anita Page
16	"NO ONE MAN"	Zazu Pitts
APR 17	"THREE WISE GIRLS"	Carole Lombard
18	"AIR EAGLE"	Jean Harlow
19	"MAD GENIUS"	Richard Bartholo
20	"TWO KINDS OF WOMEN"	John Barrymore
21	"DANCE TEAM"	Miriam Hopkins
22	"ALIAS THE BAD MAN"	James Donn
23	"WITHOUT HONOR"	N/A
24	"RACING YOUTH"	
25	"TARZAN THE APE MAN"	Harry Carey
May 26	"HATCHET MAN"	N/A
27	"SPECKLED BAND"	Johnny Weismuller
28	"BEAST OF THE CITY"	Edward G. Robinson
29	"CROWD ROARS"	Clive Brook
JUNE 30	"LADY WITH A PAST"	WALTER Huston
31	"LOCAL BAD MAN"	JAMES Cagney
32	"MAN WHO PLAYED GOD"	Constance Benn
33	"SHE WANTED A MILLIONAIRE"	Hoot Gibson
34	"PLAY GIRL"	George Arliss
35	"BIG SHOT"	Joan Bennet
36	"LETTY LYNTON"	Loretta Young
37	"ATTORNEY FOR THE DEFENSE"	Maureen O'Sullivan
July 38	"EXPERI"	Joan Crawford
39	"MYSTERY RANCH"	Edmund Lowe
		Chick Sale
		N/A

106

Chapter Twenty-Five

Bernard

Betty was planning to attend a dance held at the local Y. Stella asked Betty to take several girls with her to the dance.

"Oh, Mommie," Betty complained. "Why do you want me to do that? Those two
 girls will stop me from meeting other friends."

Stella said, "You owe it to your Aunt Evelyn. They are her friend's children. And I really don't want you to go to that dance alone."

By this time Betty had begun to think more socially and even the idea of going to a dance was evidence of her need to find a place in her life for socialization. Betty reluctantly agreed to have the two girls accompany her to the dance. It was a first experience for her two friends. Betty felt superior to these girls. They were sisters and still in high school.

When Saturday night came, she fussed with her dress and hair, which by now was long and dark brown and shining, which offset her green eyes with an Asian upturn, matching her pert nose. She was an attractive young woman but was not aware of it yet.

At the dance she joined the females on one side of the room as the males gathered on the other side. The three of them were standing in a group against the wall of the recreation hall. It was a rather drab basement, festooned with balloons and streamers. Betty's back was to the dance floor.

The girls visited the punchbowl and generally talked and giggled. The dancing began and a boy she did not know asked her to dance and she did. When she returned she was standing facing her two charges, Hilda and Joanie, two rather dull, to Betty, unattractive young women, a year or two older than she.

Suddenly, someone tapped her shoulder from behind and airily greeted her with,

"Hi ya, milk-girl!"

She turned abruptly, blushed to her hair line and found that the boy from the stoop was addressing her.

"I beg your pardon," Betty remarked. "That is not my name."

"Well, what is it?" he insisted.

"Betty Anne," she replied.

He extended his hand and said, "It really is nice to meet you at last. I'm Bernard. Dance?"

"Only if you dance with my friends first," Betty said.

"Sure," Bernard said, without blinking.

He walked them home that night. He soon became a devoted friend. He was a kind, sweet person. Stella was so happy for Betty. Bernard had graduated from high school and was not planning to go on to college. He was working for his father and older brother. It soon became apparent that Bernard and Betty were a couple and they spent time together on weekends with his group.

Bernard was nineteen and had a group of friends who were all NYU students, many in NYU's School of Dentistry. Betty was impressed by this. This group became the center of her social life for the next two years. Stella was delighted with Bernard, who knew how to talk to her and didn't mind doing so. He never asked about Martin or his whereabouts, and Stella and Betty appreciated this.

Betty began to spend time with the college group and soon realized that Bernard did not meet her intellectual needs. Somewhere, deep inside, she hungered for more. She began to juggle dates with two other beaus, Irvin, a slick, bookish intellectual with no interest in anything, but a good time, and Murray, a law student. These three boys were all eager to be her 'main beau' but each of them, were useful though, and she matured learning more about dealing with relationships. They spent time together on weekends. Soon, Bernie faded into the background. Irvin was more a friend than a romantic attachment, but Murray, bright and persistent, became the dominant male in her life for several years.

Graduation was looming. It was 1937 and a future was not too clearly in view. A major factor was the high unemployment rate as the economy had not fully recovered. Graduation was at Carnegie Hall. Stella, Henry, and Murray attended.

During all of this time, Martin would turn up periodically. He would be morose or angry and sounds of dissention began to be evident when he did come home. He stayed a while and then just as unceremoniously left. During one of these sporadic visits, he would arrive burdened with several bags of groceries. It almost seemed like peace offerings. The marriage was falling apart; Stella knew this. Betty sensed something, but Stella did not confide in Betty. She maintained a stoicism that began to color her outlook on life generally. Martin's visits were always pleasant when he arrived. He always greeted Betty and Henry warmly. Henry did not react much but Betty was delighted to see Martin. Sadly as he and Stella began to talk behind closed doors, there would be loud arguments which soon ended and Martin would leave. Betty was saddened and felt abandoned. She, too, was learning how to accept the pain quietly.

Betty was now approaching her high school graduation in January of 1933. She would become sixteen in June and was determined to become a geologist after her college years. Henry was in junior high, doing well academically, but into disciplinary trouble which occasioned Stella's visit to the school several times.

Betty graduated from high school. It was 1933. Resources were limited and Stella was alone. Martin was gone. The Larkins returned to their previous role of non-interest and non- involvement. Morey had died leaving all of his assets to Marjorie, his common-law wife. Stella wondered how she was to survive with two children to support. In 1933 there was no social security, no welfare, nothing. Their future was bleak, but Stella was strong.

With Martin out of the house, and no longer using the Hearst papers as the only source of information about world events, Betty began to question many of the happenings around the world, looking for answers. The world stage was in the throes of huge changes. Rumblings of the growing Fascist movement with its anti-Semitism and flagrant ethnic discrimination needed some answers. There was much confusion concerning the rise of this militarily discriminatory political system which seemed to capture a segment of the German population, led by a rabid paper hanger called Adolf Hitler. Concurrent with this need to spread her wings, she began to attend youth-group meetings at the Y, which often had speakers discussing the world of politics. She sometimes became so agitated by the need to resolve some thoughts that she hung around after the meeting to listen to the political talk among the young people.

One day, one of the leaders of the group approached her and urged her to join the group as a way to keep up with the changing world. She agreed and enjoyed the new friendships. She soon became the secretary and with her devotion to doing everything well, she was efficient and happy, and found a new venue for her interests and energies.

Several weeks later, she was seated on the platform taking the minutes. She glanced around the auditorium and noted that there were two young men, new to her, seated towards the back of the room.

One was a tall blond boy and the other was shorter and brown-haired. They remained for a few minutes at the end of the meeting. He, the darker haired boy, approached her at the end of the meeting and asked whether she would like to come to a party at his house the following Friday. She was surprised by the abruptness of the invitation, never having spoken to him before, but she agreed, saying that she had a previous date, but would make some other arrangements with the person involved. She needed to talk to Stella first. Betty still felt like an obedient child and always consulted with Stella as to social protocol. Stella at first seemed reluctant to allow Betty to go, but she finally gave her permission.

/ / / / / / / / / / / / / / /

Chapter Twenty-Six
No More Hearst

Betty found her relationship with Murray was losing its glitter. He was still attentive and caring, but Betty found life boring with little relief from movies or ice cream sodas. It was now 1939 and war rumors were evident. She felt an urge to become a participant. There were many activities at the local Y. She began to spend some evenings at the center. She was taking a few courses towards her Master's degree which did not require too much of her study time.

This particular Friday, Murray was studying for the bar exam. She wandered over to the Y. There was a meeting called by some youth group for "Preservation of Democracy." The subject was the anti-labor practices of the government. Strikers were beaten, cops on horses trampled workers, and bullets were fired to break the strikes.

Betty sat close to the front—eager to hear and learn. There were three people on the platform—two boys and a girl. The girl was taking notes and one of the boys looked about her age or younger. When a point was made, there was scattered applause among the attendees. Betty raised her hand and surprised herself by asking a question. A debate ensued within the audience and a confrontation occurred with the chairperson. When the meeting ended, a group stood around still discussing the fine points of the question—legislate or take direct action. Betty was asked to join which she did and soon became the note taker on the dais. Several weeks later, at the following month's meeting, Betty was seated at the table on the slightly raised platform, wearing a skirt which allowed her legs to be visible. Seated in the back row of the auditorium were two men new to Betty, but apparently known to many in attendance, because the people greeted the taller one as they entered the auditorium.

At the end of the meeting, the dark haired, shorter man, who was about twenty or twenty one, approached Betty.

"Hi, my name is Raymond. I wondered whether you were free tomorrow evening to come to a gathering at my home."

"Well, I did have a date, but I can break it. Yes, I'd be delighted to come."

She called Murray and made some lame excuse about work for school.

/ / / / / / / / / / / / / / /

Chapter Twenty-Six

Bart

Raymond lived in a small apartment building a few blocks away. She was excited to become involved with a new circle of young people who seemed to represent a more intellectually curious group. Raymond greeted her at the door and welcomed her. Standing slightly behind him was an attractive girl, whom he introduced as Lainie, his girlfriend. Betty was momentarily disappointed, thinking that, Raymond would be her date. He then led her over to the tall blond guy, Bart. Raymond then disappeared into the kitchen. At first she did not understand, but then soon saw that Ray was acting on Bart's behalf. She soon realized that this young man was different. Bart was intense and over time became persistent in his pursuit of her time and affection. When she was first introduced to him, and they made eye contact, it was almost mesmerizing, and she felt as if she was losing her usual self assurance. The electricity flowed between them on unseen wires. *What is going on here?* she thought. *What magic did this young Adonis have, which overwhelms me so?*

He, in turn was enchanted by her looks, her intelligence, and her vivacious personality. He knew that this young woman would play an important part in his life. He was a leader, charismatic and wise. He was devoted to improving the lot of the downtrodden, the poor, the young people, the farmers—any group whose lives and work were attacked by the 'establishment'. He would join forces with the trade unions, the student activists on campuses, in fact, any group whose concepts were in line with the majority of the coalition. Franklin D. Roosevelt was in office and seemed to respond to the people's agitation for better conditions. This became the central concern of Bart's life.

She knew that Bart was so different. She missed him so much when he was not there with her. She began to sense that these feelings were deeper than friendship and they then knew that they loved each other very much.

He lived with his parents, an older brother and sister. He was the baby or as their personalized nicknames went, he was the 'pup', his brother was the 'mutt', his sister was the 'girl', and his mother was the 'frau', a reflection of the German language which the parents used frequently. Somehow, the father escaped a nickname. He was a very talented craftsman. He owned a store in upper Manhattan. He was proficient in using, designing, and installing any form of glass. He made several of the leaded glass windows in St. Patrick's Cathedral. Sadly, he suffered from diabetes and a heart condition, which Bart inherited when he reached his forties. His father succumbed to a coronary attack in 1940. The frau had a small notions store which sustained her economically. She suffered from Meniere's Syndrome resulting in deafness and fainting spells. Betty and Bart were soon enveloped in a serious relationship. All of the other boys seemed to be relegated to a back burner and then no longer significant in Betty's life.

Chapter Twenty-Seven
College

Betty was enrolled in the City University at the all girls college and Bart was also at the University, but at the all-boys school Betty was majoring in Geology with a Biology minor, along with teacher training courses. Bart began to court her extensively and soon they were a 'couple'. Stella was not happy about this at all. He was a poor boy and that was not in her game plan for Betty. Once more, due to the exigencies of funds, Stella and the children had to move again. This time to a smaller apartment with only two bedrooms and Henry slept on the couch in the living room. However, there was a dining room, so there was some public space. It was on 54th Street, a corner building, and all the other houses on the street were private.

One day when Betty was still in high school, concerned that due to the family's low financial situation, she was not sure that Stella could afford to allow her to go to college. She felt she would do as most of her friends did, find a job and maybe continue studying at night. This particular day, late in her senior year, with her college applications already mailed, she came home to find Stella sitting in the living room, certainly a rarity.

"Betty, come and sit down, I want to talk to you. I am going to tell you about an incident, which you may or may not remember. We were in the country visiting Aunt Janette. Before bed time, we went out on the porch, and I asked you to say goodnight to the animals and the plants, which you dutifully did. This particular evening, you asked to say goodnight to the stars and of course you did. Suddenly, you said, 'What is a star?' I don't know," I responded. "What is a star made of?" you asked. "I don't know," I replied. "What keeps them up there?" "I don't know." And then you began to cry.

At the moment when this incident had originally occurred, Stella had made a silent promise to herself that she would never allow any question of Betty's to go unanswered. Stella then bought several books for Betty and most of her questions were answered when she was just five years old. This is a look at the internal struggles that Stella endured during her entire life but never revealed to anyone. However, her decision to allow Betty to go to college, instead of to work, gives us a glimpse into her thinking.

"Therefore, you are going to go to college," Stella exultantly replied.

As a consequence, Betty soon studied astronomy in depth and often related this incident in later years to her children. Betty knew that it was a difficult financial time. As she began her college education, Stella gave Betty twenty-five cents each day. Ten cents was for carfare, by subway, from Brooklyn to Manhattan and back. The remaining fifteen cents was for lunch money in the student cafeteria. Betty recalled that the Friday menu was fish cakes and spaghetti and tea, or coffee or milk. She never questioned this frugality. She focused on the importance of education.

"We will manage somehow," Stella lovingly consoled Betty.

Each day that she attended classes at college, this short interchange kept cropping up at the least expected moments. The parable remained with her into her later years. Although Stella never took a course in Parenting or Child Psychology, she had the intelligence, wisdom and love to understand how important it was for Betty to pursue her dream. She graduated from the City University in January 1937, one of the youngest in her class at 19 ½.

/ / / / / / / / / / / / / / /

Martin   1951

Stella & Benjy 1978

Morton 1898

Claire 1898

Irvin   1920

Martin 1934 (Montana)

Stella 1985

Henry 1975

Betty 1968

Betty 1928

Chapter Twenty-Eight
The Visit

Several years later, when Betty and Bart had become a 'couple', they were both sitting in the dining room on a hot summer Sunday, talking, when the doorbell rang, Betty went to the door and Martin was standing there with two tall bags of groceries almost obscuring his face. His face looked bloated and his eyes very red.

"Hi, Boopsie, how have you been?"

His greeting seemed as if he had just come home from work when in fact it had been almost six months since he had been home. He put the groceries on the table and Betty introduced Bart. After a few words of banal conversation, Martin disappeared into the kitchen with the groceries and soon, a door was slammed and loud voices came from the back bedroom. Bart and Betty were uncomfortable, but tried very hard to ignore the arguing that was obviously occurring. Within ten minutes, Martin came back into the dining room, his brown hat in hand. He came around the table, shook hands with Bart, gave Betty a hug, and opened the door.

"See you soon, Boopsie. We'll be in touch."

It was the last time Betty was to see Martin.

/ / / / / / / / / / / / / / /

Chapter Twenty-Nine
Accident #4

Several months later, now on a wintry Sunday, Betty and Bart were alone at Betty's. Henry was playing basketball in Connecticut with a team sponsored by a local hardware store. This was Henry's current passion. Stella was visiting a friend in Queens. There was much to talk about. This was late 1940, and a year before Pearl Harbor. A dear friend of Bart's, George, who, wanting to contribute to the fight against Fascism, joined the Abraham Lincoln Brigade, an international volunteer army. The brigade was in Spain, helping the civilians fight against the dictatorship of Francisco Franco. George died there at the Ebro River, defending democracy. He was nineteen years old. The isolationist policies of the US and the UK neglected to see the Civil War in Spain as the possible precursor to the conflagration soon to descend destructively over all of Europe and into the Pacific. The allies stood by, watched and did nothing.

Several months later, now on a wintry Sunday afternoon, at about mid afternoon, the phone rang. Bart answered. His monosyllabic responses and eventual silence caused Betty, busy in the kitchen, to enquire as to the problem.

"Please," Bart said, "Don't be upset and sit down," he urged quietly.

Betty was shocked to see Bart's blanched look on his usually ruddy cheeks. "That was Barney, Ernst's overseer. "There had been an accident at Ernie's place and he wants us to get there quickly."

Betty and Bart arrived at Ernie's place, to find police and fire vehicles blocking access to the street. The faint odor of truck exhaust, hung precariously in the air. The garage doors were wide open revealing several trucks, standing immobile. A man's body in a dark blue overcoat was lying face down on the floor.

Between sobs, and in a quivering voice, Betty said, "Yes, that is my uncle, Ernst Danvers."

The police ruled it an accidental death. The police reasoned that Ernst had come in to rev up the motors of the trucks, to be ready for Monday morning. The cops indicated that the small entry door had been open, but was blown shut by a gust of wind, as Ernie probably went downstairs to the bathroom. To Betty, this whole event was eerie in its similarity to the accidental death of Grandma Danvers, who died as a gust of wind blew out the gas-lit heater in the office in Rockaway.

Ernie must have been aware of the exhaust, as he was found with a wet towel, covering his mouth and nose. The designation of an accident was official, but Betty and Bart felt it could have been a suicide, due to the intractable role played by Elise, Ernie's wife, in not releasing him from their failed marriage.

Elise took over the business and fired Henry. Stella was back in financial trouble. The family moved once again to a smaller less desirable space.

When financial disaster had loomed, Stella had reached out to her brother Ernst, who had had a thriving business and by hiring Henry was able to use this ploy to help Stella and the children survive. Ernst had provided financial and emotional help to Stella without revealing this information to Elise, his wife.

Martin's attempt to provide some financial assistance soon stopped as he deteriorated into an alcoholic. Almost all contact ceased.

Ernst had followed his father's work life. He worked for Morey, but soon tired of the endless bickering and Morey's need to control and micro manage every aspect of the workday. As he grew older, he had no interest in further education, as the need to work was paramount. He tried working for other companies, but the itch to be independent grew. He was a decent, quiet, and ambitious person. He met and married Elise which was a surprising choice, as everyone remarked. She was neither attractive in appearance nor pleasant in demeanor. Perhaps this was exacerbated by her deformity. She had a sizeable scapular protrusion, probably due to a severe kyphoscoliosis. In common parlance, she had a large 'hump' protruding from the left shoulder. Obviously, nothing had been done in her pre-teen and teenage years. And this orthopedic abnormality was literally the family's accepted burden. Her family so delighted with Ernst that he wallowed in the affection and admiration heaped on him, which he needed and had not received from his father. The Fortrells were so happy with Ernst because of his sweet personality and their joy at Elise finding a husband.

The Fortrells were delighted by Ernie's entrance into the family, but they never were very friendly to Stella and the children. Stella tried to reach out to Elise but was not too successful. Elise considered Stella a blight and a shameful disgrace in the family. Due to this distance between Elise and Stella, Ernst kept his genuine love and concern for Stella and the children to himself. He eventually opened a business at Bush Terminal. He had one truck but soon expanded to several more. The garage and storage area was on the Brooklyn waterfront facing Manhattan. It was becoming a growing port of entry for cargo ships and all the ancillary businesses that dealt with incoming and outgoing cargo. Adjacent to Ernie's establishment, there were a few remaining residential buildings. A recently arrived Italian family called Gaetano, had a young son called Bernardo, but initiated by the truck drivers as Barney, who became the de facto custodian of Ernie's business site. He worked as watchman and general maintenance man. He kept the sidewalk clean of litter and shoveled the snow when needed. He was devoted to "the Boss."

Elise worked for a while after the marriage. She had been the bookkeeper for one of Ernie's customers. She soon was pregnant and a beautiful daughter, Cora, became Ernie's delight. A few years later Morton was born. Ernie was a devoted father and husband. Friction between Elise and Ernie began when Cora was about eight years old.

From the very beginning of Elise's entry into the family, there developed coldness between Elise and Stella. Stella always felt close to Elise's children, but Elise never warmed to Betty and Henry. When Martin no longer was a part of the scene, Elise's distance grew, as she did not look favorably at either Stella or Martin. But Ernest torn by his love for his children, but angered and saddened by Stella's plight chose to deny Elise any information concerning his relationship to Stella. Stella had no choice but to turn to him for help. He proposed a plan. Henry would come to work for him after school and Saturdays and what he earned plus some extra funds would allow Stella to survive. There was no other safety net.

131

Most of the reason was Elise's mother's interference in his life, which subsequently led to his unwillingness to come home when the Fortrells were there. On one of these evenings, he went to visit a customer about some error in a payment. He had talked to the bookkeeper before and was impressed with her quiet knowledge of the business and her gracious manner. This evening, she was about to leave for the day and he suggested they go to dinner, and he would explain the problem then. This soon developed into an 'affair' and he found himself deeply involved with this woman. He approached Elise with a request for a separation and eventual divorce.

Her reply was "No, I'll never allow you to marry your whore."

He moved out, miserable at the prospect of only seeing his children on weekends. He surreptitiously opened a bank account in Stella's name and made periodic deposits, anticipating a possible complication in the hopefully eventual divorce proceedings. Stella never knew of this account.

Ernst was becoming disenchanted with the Fortrell family's constant presence and intrusion in his life. Elise, his wife, did not understand his attitude. He maintained his obligation to his family, but his heart was turning away.

Stella had turned to Ernst and despite the turmoil in his married life, he was willing to help. He hired Henry, who enjoyed working, after school and Saturdays, as the excuse to provide sustenance for Stella. Henry was fascinated by the activity at Ernie's place. He was more interested in the office activity than the physical work in the warehouse and garage. He did his work well and Ernst noted his willingness to learn and work. It seemed to foreshadow his adult work ethic.

Ernst had been helping to support Stella and the children, as Martin's contribution dwindled to almost nothing. At this point in time around the early 40's, there still were not any safety nets to help families in need. Stella still did not see employment as a possible answer for herself. She appealed to Ernst, and he was willing to help with no information to Elise. He hired Henry to work at the garage, doing odd jobs, as an after-school and Saturday work time. Sometimes, Henry would take his red wagon and pick up newspapers and sell it at the junkyard.

It seemed almost 'de rigeur' for Stella and her children to constantly face the roller coaster ride of uncertainty in terms of financial insecurity. In these days (2017), we cannot imagine an existence of this volatility. But we do know that in parts of the world, today and in the recent past, there are still millions of people suffering from not only minimal financial resources, but illnesses and needless loss of life, especially children. Has Society improved? Always, this is a troubling question with the amazing technological advances and the minimal personal ones.

/ / / / / / / / / / / / / / /

Chapter Thirty
The Padre

Joe had been determined to rid his organization of Martin because of Martin's poor results in securing additional business. He also knew that Martin was resorting to alcohol. He knew that by these actions, with his incessant drinking, and his constant argumentative manner, he didn't need to do anything that would antagonize Evie. Joe knew that soon, in fact, very soon, Martin would self destruct and he, Joe, would come out of these troubles cleanly and without a scar.

Martin still used Philadelphia as the base of his operation. He now became responsible for sales in the area of Pennsylvania, Ohio and Illinois. He was still selling chemicals for farm use as well as a catalytic agent to speed up the process of manufacturing steel. This was a major industry, especially in Philadelphia and Pittsburgh, and in the Youngstown, Ohio steel mills. (It is strange to realize that those industries along with the auto manufacturing sites, have been decimated by the owner corporations seeking cheaper labor offshore since the 1970's.)

Martin was becoming disenchanted with the non-existent glamour of his ascendancy into the world of business. He began to neglect calling on clients, ending his work day earlier and earlier. He would find his way to the nearest bar and spend the evening drinking. He knew his diabetes would suffer, so he managed most times to control the quantity and did eat to soak up the booze. He then would go to a local hotel, sit in the lobby, smoke a bit and wander off to bed.

Soon his income began to drop. He sent less money, with excuses, to Stella and began to relocate to cheaper hotels. One night he just couldn't face the place in which he was staying. He wandered into an auction house flopped into a back row and watched the procedure. He was intrigued watching the role of the shills, who cleverly raised the bids. He kept falling asleep and had to be roused and urged to leave.

He wrote to Stella urging her to forget him, take good care of the children, but to send a few dollars, as he was just not making enough to get by. He was now down to almost no work and spending most of his time either drinking or sleeping it off. One night he was so depressed, he decided to drink himself into a stupor. He was forced out of the bar he was in and he just couldn't make it to the hotel. He did not remember the sequence, but assumed that he was so drunk that he just collapsed in the street and fell asleep. The next thing he recalled is that he awoke in a bed with clean linens, and soon a nurse and a minister arrived and he realized he was in a dry out ward. This was in the late 30's and alcoholics were treated as patients, not criminals.

The padre sat down and took Martin's hands in his own and said, "Young man, you have been pretty sick. The good people here are trying to bring you back to good health. Will you give them your help?"

"Yeah, sure. How long have I been here?" Martin casually responded.

"Well, just long enough for us to feel that you are ready to go back to whatever you were doing. We tried to stabilize your diabetes. As you probably know, alcohol in your system could be a warning sign of serious medical problems. We urge you to be very careful. We wish you all the best."

Martin was so grateful for the interest shown by the padre that he promised to be a good Catholic and go to Mass. With that admonition, he was discharged and his clothing was returned to him along with a few dollars.

He walked out into the sunshine with a firm resolution to stop drinking and tried to come up with some scenario to think of his future. He did remember where he had last slept and returned to that hotel. He was hoping that they had emptied his room of its few personal items and saved them, especially his Boston Bag. The desk clerk remembered him and had miraculously saved and stored his personal items. The black clerk was a recovered alcoholic and felt sympathy for a kindred soul. Martin gave the clerk the few dollars he had received and retrieved his stuff.

Martin went to the bus station and rented a safety box and stashed his belongings. He found the cash he had kept behind the lining in the suitcase for just such an emergency. He then went for a haircut and shave to freshen his appearance. He had lost some weight and felt good. He decided to return to the auction house to see if he could earn a few bucks as a shill before he decided what to do.

The owners were less than enthusiastic as they remembered him as the drunk asleep in the back row.

Martin said, "Give me a week or two and if I don't shape up, I'll leave."

He soon became an effective shill. He was smart and looked the part with his flair for a well-dressed fake. He soon tired of this job with its fakery and knew that he was capable of much more. He needed to leave this place with its bad memories. He thought of going to Pittsburgh, which he knew slightly from his late lamented foray into the world of sales. Joe had washed his hands of helping him. His family considered him a loser and Stella no longer considered him a worthy father or husband. He knew that he was alone in his quest for survival. He decided to head west and picked Chicago as a possible place to stop.

/ / / / / / / / / / / / / / /

Chapter Thirty-One
Chicago

Stella had said that Martin did not project a proper image of a concerned parent. Sadly and unfortunately, he agreed. He walked to the local bus terminal and took the bus to Philadelphia headed for Chicago. While in transit, he felt almost euphoric in his sudden freedom. He felt almost no remorse or even a tinge of guilt by his willful separation from his past and family. In fact, he felt that he had been victimized by Joseph and rejected by Stella for conditions that he considered no fault of his own. He was feeling truly heroic. This apparent escape from reality began to serve him well. Whether this was a circumstantial effort to cope with his current environment, or a severe breakdown in his ethical and moral mores, or even a physical deterioration of his brain due to alcoholism remains a question only answerable by conjecture, as no chemical or medical evidence is available, only what is indicated by his actions.

Once in Chicago, he knew he had to find work. As this was the early 40's there still were remnants of the depression of the late 20's and jobs were not plentiful. At the bus station, he went to the Traveler's Aid booth. These booths were in all the major bus and train stations. This organization did what its title indicated. It tried to assist travelers to find food and shelter. He reluctantly asked their help. He knew that white-collar work would not be open for him, as he had no real training. They sent him to an employment agency, where a niche opened for him...hospitals.

He took a job as a surgical orderly. He wore either white or green surgical scrubs in the operating rooms. He did the post op cleanup, helped the nurses, sterilized the instruments, familiarized himself with the surgical procedures, and listened to the talk among the doctors.

Martin was a bright man and a quick learner. He managed to explore the building, often wandering to other departments and helping in the emergency room when he was off duty. He had no social life and did not seem to want to seek it. He had difficulty falling asleep as some latent unhappiness and thoughts of Betty and the past still kept him awake. He began to frequent the medical library and soon acquired some minimal information on the cause and treatments for many diseases. He became fascinated with the patient care for infectious diseases. Ideas began to percolate in his mind with the possibility of pursuing this stream of work – medicine,

He stayed at the hospital for about a year and a half, but once again, he began to feel the need to move. He had made no personal attachments. He went out with a few male colleagues for an occasional dinner. He carefully avoided any alcohol, always fearful of its consequences. He quietly gave notice of his intent to leave. His careful excuse indicated the need for his presence in Florida to care for a relative who was quite ill. It was a reasonable excuse and a simple ploy to arrange to leave without any lasting connections.

He had thought about his future and decided that this time he would seek out a small town in a less populous state. He headed toward Montana. Once again he was in transit, but this time, as he had some money squirreled away, he took a train to Billings. As the scenic

Northwest passed by he once again became thoughtful. He missed Betty very much and it was hard for him to see young children without a sadness flowing over him. He managed to always think that he was not the cause of the troubles. He was the victim. This jolted him back to the situation in hand. He now had to face a very new situation which, as yet, he had not clearly thought about.

/ / / / / / / / / / / / / / /

Chapter Thirty-Two
Stella

Stella was totally occupied with maintaining some semblance of equilibrium in the lives of the children and herself. She was naturally distressed at the turn of events in her young life, which represented a loss of support and loss of the presence of a father and husband. However, from somewhere in the depth of her being, she was determined to sweep away any remaining remnants of love and caring for her husband and lover. He was guilty of destroying her stability and her home, forcing her children to be bereft of a father, and leaving the three of them without any visible means of support. She was not willing to forgive. She would never forget. Yet she was determined to make a life for her children and herself. This grit and willful determination colored her entire life. She knew she had to learn to be independent. She could not rely on family, especially the Danzigs, who considered her the perpetrator of all the ills that had fallen on Martin. Her parents were gone, and only Ernst, her younger brother, had been on the horizon. She worked hard and life, as difficult as it was, remained on a level sustainable by Ernst's support.

Betty was totally absorbed with school. She continued to be involved in learning and spent all of her time devoted to it. What bothered Betty, but not Henry as he seemed to be totally occupied with his active athletic life, was Stella's manner of dealing with Martin's absence. Henry enjoyed his work with Ernst. Betty was disturbed by the way Stella managed to explain Martin's absence to her family.

Stella kept up the pretense that Martin still was a presence in their lives. In response to the question frequently posed by one of the aunts: "...*and how is Martin?*" she would respond with a flair:

"Oh, he is doing just fine. He is traveling and doesn't get back home very often. We speak on the phone and, of course, he sends money."

This was a clear and bald lie. She had learned well over the years of her marriage that leaving hard hurtful facts unsaid was less painful than exposing herself and children to comments, exasperating sympathies, and behind the door snickering. Although the family and she knew that what she explained was not true, everyone played the game.

Everyone, that is, except Henry and Betty. Henry seemed unscathed and did not seem to show any signs of missing the presence of his father. But for Betty, it was different. She was hurt, felt sad and neglected. She missed the hugs, the playful teasing and affection which Martin shared with her. She seemed to have been totally enmeshed in his warmth, charisma, and genuine love.

She felt lost and abandoned. Stella just could not fill the void. She loved her children dearly, but she needed all her energy in the struggle for their survival. She did her best to shield them from the disastrous circumstances of their current existence.

/ / / / / / / / / / / / / / / / /

Chapter Thirty-Three

Graduation

Graduation for Betty was pending and Betty was to graduate in January 1937 from the City University. She was one of the youngest graduates at nineteen and one half years old. The economy was still recovering from the Great Depression. She knew that even with a degree in Geology, the prospects for employment seemed dim.

Stella, Henry, and Bart attended the graduation exercises held at Carnegie Hall. Soon after graduation, she noticed an ad in the college paper asking for recent graduates in Geology to apply to Standard Oil Company of NY (SOCONY), the precursor to EXXON Mobil. The positions were for a mining exploration in Chile. Only one other student, Pearl, and Betty planned to apply.

The two young graduates hoped this position would be their ticket out into the world of work, which they had dreamed about. For both, it would be a leap out of poverty as well as an adventure in another land, another culture, another society.

As they entered the employment office, they approached the reception desk. Seated behind the high counter sat a rather unshaven man, with a cigarette dangling from his lips and, beside him was a half empty cup of coffee and an ashtray filled with stubs of many cigarettes. There also were several donuts, one half-eaten staining the papers with greasy spots.

Betty was just about to request directions, but was quickly stopped before she uttered a word.

"Huh, secretaries, over there," as the man behind the desk pointed to another desk behind him.

"No, we are applying for the field geologist job as advertised," Betty said.

He burst into loud laughter. "You...in the field...not possible. We don't hire women," the man behind the desk derisively responded.

"But we are just as qualified as the male applicants," Betty insisted.

"We couldn't let chicks like you among all those hungry men. Y'understand, NO CHICKS. Y'see, I don't trust the guys....ha ha ha. And besides, only one toilet. Git the picture?"

"That's no problem. When I get home, I have my mother, my father, and my brother and we only have one toilet," Betty explained.

They knew they were beaten and sadly they left.

Betty returned to school and lamented to Prof. Lehnerts, and he responded with words she remembered all the years of her long life.

He said, "College education merely trains you how to learn. That is all. The rest you do outside."

Chapter Thirty-Four
The Dental Lab

Betty continued studying in the evening and took the next available job as a lab technician in a dental lab owned by a dentist, who also thought he owned her.

After working there for a few weeks, she noticed that the dentist would come up to the bench where she was working and pat her head, or give her a squeeze around her shoulders. She would move away but he persisted. Then one late afternoon, he gave her a peck on the cheek. This time she confronted him and asked him to please stop. She felt that his fatherliness was being overworked.

He said, "Don't be so angry. There is no harm done."

He then encircled her waist with his both hands and pushed her towards the supply closet which was open and forced her inside the small space. She struggled to get away, but he began to kiss and fondle her. She managed to get into a better position and she kneed him in the groin and pulled away. She could hear him saying in a pained tone,

"I only wanted you to come away with me for the weekend conference up at the Hotel Concord."

She ran down the stairs into the street and into a coffee shop on the corner. She was frightened and perplexed. The waitress, whom she knew, mouthed the word, "*Coffee?*" and Betty nodded.

After about ten minutes, she knew that there was nothing she could do and no one to whom she could relate this incident. This was

1940 and there was no legal or quasi-legal safety net. She needed the job and knew she had to return there. It took many years before sexual abuse was talked about and dealt with. It made Betty very alert to these problems. Although Bart did understand, she did not want anyone else to be involved. She returned to work and strangely, the abuse stopped.

As the Second World War escalated in Europe, there were forces in the US which proposed isolation. Most of the American people knew that somehow we would have to be involved. Many Americans felt that we could not allow the infamous attacks against minorities, especially the Jews, to go on. December 7, 1941, the attack against Pearl Harbor settled the question. However, there were events prior to that date which concerned Bart and Betty. The young couple knew that they wanted to marry, but when and how were difficult to answer.

As Betty was still at the lab, she asked the dentist if she could purchase some dental gold so that she could cast marriage rings.

He was very gracious and said, "It is my present to you."

After work on Saturday afternoon, she began the process of carving the rings in wax, then applying a special compound. She took the gold which came in small flat pieces and placed them on a centrifuge and with the blowtorch began the melting process.

Just as she was ready to release the centrifuge and allow the molten gold to be forced into the hollowed form, the phone rang and she was momentarily distracted. She did complete the release and answered the phone. As she returned to the bench she looked down and saw that her stockings were ripped. She could see that there were

146

some burn spots on her legs. She called a doctor in the building and went down to have him look at her leg. He said that the heat had vaporized the gold and seared the flesh without any pain.

"Just tell your fiancé that he's getting a gal with gold in her legs."

However, the rings were made successfully.

/ / / / / / / / / / / / / / /

Chapter Thirty-Five

Hitchhiking

It was now early 1941 and Bart was to be drafted in April. The war had heated up in the European Theater and the draft was instituted.

Betty and Bart knew that a wedding with family was not what they wanted because of family objections and secondly the war. So they enlisted the secret services of Bart's cousin who was a physician who drew blood for the pre-marital test required in New York.

With the certificate and license in hand, they began the trek to the marriage bureau every Saturday morning with no success. The lines were long and the couples were many. They tried in Manhattan with similar results. On the Saturday before Bart's induction, they were desperate. Bart had a plan.

They took the train to 241 Street and hitched a ride on a truck carrying chairs to a wedding hall. They got off at the first stop in Westchester. Betty and Bart went into a cigar store and checked the yellow pages for a Justice of the Peace. They took the first one—Jefferson Browder—and called and walked into the quaint Victorian home with a wraparound porch facing the river. The door was opened by a wrinkled woman of about seventy years. They were led into an overstuffed parlor with a fireplace and mantle.

A short, slightly distorted man with a kindly face and heavy horn-rimmed glasses stood with his back to the fireplace and motioned Betty and Bart forward. The woman who opened the door was the

JP's wife and she was the necessary witness. The ceremony was short and the JP asked the newly wed couple to kiss and indulged his privilege and pecked Betty on the cheek.

After the ceremony, the two left—happy, but bewildered and concerned about their future. They returned to New York and rented a room in the Hotel Holland on 42nd Street. They went to the Automat for dinner. They bought a copy of the Times, and returned to their honeymoon suite. It was April 12, 1941. Bart was drafted on April 17, eight months before Pearl Harbor.

/ / / / / / / / / / / / / /

Chapter Thirty-Six

En Route

Martin's thoughtful reverie was soon broken by the announcement that they had reached Billings. He went to a local map of the area and talked to the ticket master as to the size of some of the farming towns close by. He selected one which seemed to have a population under 1000. His informant also told him that there was a dentist in town but no medical doctor. You had to go about fifteen miles to get the nearest doctor. He thought he had found the perfect spot. He saw a small garage nearby and went and found an old jalopy which he purchased for fifty dollars. He filled the car with gas, and with a local map went to seek out a new temporary home.

He drove up the main street, cozily called Home Street, and went to the small hotel nearby, took a room, and left his luggage. He remembered seeing a sign at the hardware store in the center of town, indicating an apartment for rent. He was greeted warmly by the storekeeper who said the apartment was above the store. They walked up the one flight of stairs and Martin was delighted. He paid the rent in advance and asked where he could find a bed, dresser, etc. He was told to go out to Cooper's Farm, whose owner had just passed away and they were trying to sell the household goods. He bought a bed with linens, a dresser and mirror, two small kitchen cabinets, a desk and a few chairs, a few pots and dishes. One of the Cooper sons drove behind him in a pickup, and they both brought the stuff upstairs.

Martin knew he was on a silent track to obliterate any memory of his past life and merely to concentrate on the here and now, and just maybe a future. He knew there were dangers, but he proceeded to effect his silent plan to hide behind a new identity and activity. He hung a small sign at the doorway in the street, which said M.B. LANG, Medical Care. He carefully refrained from using MD. He outfitted the rooms, one as a small office with a partition and the examining room behind the partition and then his private quarters of a small kitchen and bedroom. The bathroom was in the hallway. He felt comfortable and fairly secure.

The next day the hardware-store owner, Sam Walsh, called him from the doorway and asked if he could come up. He had scraped his elbow and cut his finger reaching for a rough-cut file from an upper shelf.

Martin very graciously greeted him and asked him to come into the treatment room. He ceremoniously washed his hands from a pitcher and basin sitting on a counter. He cleaned the wounds, applied some antiseptic and then bandaged the wounds. Martin urged Mr. Walsh to keep it dry, but to return in three days. The fee was three dollars for the two visits. Mr. Walsh told all of his customers of the efficient way Doc Lang had treated him.

A few days later, a woman came slowly up the stairs. She carefully entered the office. She appeared to be in her sixties. She was wearing a housedress, a patterned cotton dress, with a high neckline trimmed in lace. She wore a straw hat with wisps of grey hair peeking out from under the brim.

"Excuse me sir, but are you the Medical Man?"

"Yes, I am, and how can I help you?"

"Well, you see, sir, it ain't for me. It is for my grandson and he ain't right likely to come up here."

"Is he downstairs?" Martin asked. She nodded her head.

"Well, let's go down and bring him up."

They both went down and Martin kept looking around for a carriage, but didn't see anybody.

'I'm sorry, but he ain't here."

"Oh, yes, sir, he's standing right next to you."

Martin turned to his left, and standing near him was a tall lanky young boy of about seventeen, grinning sheepishly. Trying not to laugh, Martin convinced the boy that there would not be any real pain.

. "This is Clarence, my grandson."

In the examining room, the boy proceeded to explain that he and his friend, Jasper, were tussling friendly-like until Jasper gave him a hard push and he fell against an old fence and a rusted nail dug into his arm. It bled and he went home and granny washed it, but it didn't look good so they came here.

Once again he remembered the procedure from the emergency room and carefully tended to the wound. As this was before WWII, there were no antibiotics, so alcohol and iodine had to suffice.

"You keep this dry and no fighting and come back in a week, and I'll take a look. That will be four dollars for the two visits."

"Thank you, Doc, very much."

After almost nine months of treating the minor ills of the local farm community, Martin soon became a respected member of the area. He was greeted warmly as Doc Lang, which he neither applauded nor resisted. He soon realized that his position in the town made him fearful of having his identity exposed. Although he thoroughly enjoyed the role he was playing, he felt he could do better.

He decided it was time to move on. He began to leave hints about his elderly relatives in Georgia who needed care. He arranged with his landlord, Sam Walsh, to take the furnishings and sell them and keep the money in lieu of the last two month's rent. He took the remaining medical supplies with him as well as the sign. He withdrew all monies from the bank. He felt he left no trace of his having been there.

/ / / / / / / / / / / / / / /

Chapter Thirty-Seven
Denver

Once again he headed to the bus station, changed his mind, and went to the railroad station. He bought a ticket to Denver on the 8:00am train, but decided to leave earlier at dawn and take the freighter which had fewer passengers. With the sun barely on the horizon he closed the office door placed his hat at a jaunty angle and slowly went down the creaky stairs carrying his Boston Bag and another suitcase. Without a backward glance he left, walking directly to the train station.

He settled in Denver in a hotel for a few weeks. He went to a local hospital posing as a salesman from Johnson & Johnson to acquaint himself with any new pharmaceuticals that might be of use in a hospital. He bought a new sport jacket and some shirts to properly reflect his now more affluent status. He was very adept at this camouflage. He loved good clothes and a smart look.

He sat in the lobby smoking a cigar when he noticed a young girl who startled him. She looked to be about Betty's age and this triggered poignant thoughts of the sweet times he had had with his child. His only connection to the past was the loss of the affection of his child. He wondered if she ever thought of him. He had to stop. It was no good to dwell on. He knew that any stress could exacerbate his diabetes. He had been warned many times. He sat contemplating his next move westward.

He remembered that one of the men who had financed Joe's

enterprises had said that there were a few pharmaceutical firms in the Los Angeles area that were in competition with his firm. Martin thought that with his training at the hospital and his stint as a medical practitioner as well as his knowledge of salesmanship, he could easily work in pharmaceuticals. He had to develop a reasonable explanation for his being in California and soon his next fantasy story began to develop silently.

He arrived in Los Angeles, quite content with his sojourn from Philadelphia. He felt good physically. His diabetes and weight were under control and he looked forward to the next adventure in his odyssey.

He asked questions at the information booth in the railway station to find his way to a less affluent part of the city and there were many. He eventually reached a fairly modest hotel and rented a room. He decided to pump himself up a bit, got a haircut and manicure, bought a new sport jacket, shirts and ties. To strangers whom he met, he carefully allowed the impression that he was recovering from a tragedy which he was loathe to talk about. He also let the information float about that he was Doc Lang.

On the activity board at the hotel, he saw a notice of a meeting of the Elks, a fraternal do-good organization known for its assistance to the impoverished. He decided to attend. An appeal for volunteers was made and he joined a committee that helped to act as a Big Brother to young boys, a sort of Boy Scout group. He had spent a short time in Montana helping with a Boy Scout group. He, however, indicated that he had had experience in Ada, Oklahoma.

One of the members, John Hansen, became friendly, and tried

to get at the truth from this enigmatic, yet charismatic, man. Hansen was the director of sales for one of the smaller liquor companies and asked Martin to come and work for him in sales. Martin, at first pretended to be reluctant to take the offer, as he said to John that he was still suffering from the loss of his practice to fire and theft. He told Hansen that he was unmarried and in need of a new life. He came to the Sunshine State to regain his confidence and his health. He related the saga of both his diabetes and his ongoing cardiac condition.

Hansen assigned him to a district where it was easy to sell booze. It was not difficult to sell the product, but it was difficult to deal with the big name competitors. Martin worked long hours determined to make a mark. He was successful and Hansen was delighted with his progress. Martin moved to an upscale hotel and fiddled with the idea of getting an apartment of his own. He used his signature, Doc Lang, and it soon became an accepted fact that this man lost his practice, but retained his interest and understanding of medical information. He gave talks to the young boys in the Big Brothers group about potential opportunities in medicine and allied fields. This was coupled with his improved financial situation. He was promoted to Assistant Manager of Sales, and became a figure on the dinner circuit. Doc Lang had arrived!

/ / / / / / / / / / / / / / / /

Chapter Thirty-Eight
Fort Bragg, NC

After Betty and Bart's marriage and honeymoon, they returned to their respective homes, not revealing the marriage to either family. On the 17th of April, 1941, Bart was drafted into the US Army and from Fort Dix in New Jersey went to Fayetteville, North Carolina and became a private in the Field Artillery Division located at Fort Bragg. As this was months away from December 7th and the attack on Pearl Harbor, the soldiers were merely playing at war. They didn't have rifles or ammunition. They used branches of trees and bags of flour to simulate artillery fire.

Each soldier earned twenty-one dollars per month, and cigarettes in the Post Exchange cost eight cents. Bart adjusted readily to the routines but missed Betty and called her, frequently, reversing charges. She was determined to visit and in July when she had a two week vacation from the lab, she decided to go down to Fort Bragg. Bart would arrange for a furnished room in town where she could stay.

By this time, Bart had written a letter to each Mother announcing their marriage, so that Betty's visit would be proper. Stella was not surprised, nor too happy, but accepting. Bella, Bart's mother, was dismayed. She said a proper introduction to the family was needed and she would have a reception at her home whenever Bart could come home. The difference in attitude of the two Moms was always a chasm between them. Stella considered herself so much more modern and Bella, old fashioned.

Betty was very excited at the prospect of seeing Bart and she finally arrived at Penn Station to take a rickety old train called the Atlantic Coastal Line, which had wooden uncomfortable seats. Dragging her suitcase and with ticket in hand, she began to scour the cars, but could not find a vacant seat. She eventually wended her way towards the back of the train and noticed that the last car had some empty seats. She walked towards that car when an elderly black conductor attempted to stop her.

"Don't think you should go into that car, Miss."

"And why not?" she replied

"Well, you all take a look in there and you'll see why."

She proceeded to do just that and realized that the train was almost fully occupied with black women and a few elderly men.

"But there are empty seats, so I'm going in."

She walked in covered with questioning gazes from all the occupants. She tried to smile, but no one responded. She decided on a seat next to a young woman holding a small infant in her arms. The woman moved slightly away from Betty. They sat quietly and the train began to move. It was not a comfortable ride. The wooden seats with slats were not meant for human bodies and there didn't seem to be shock absorbers as the rattle and swerving from side to side was unnerving. Suddenly, the young woman turned to Betty and asked in a direct way,

"You nigra?"

Betty laughed and said, "I am dark skinned because I lived at the beach when I was very young."

"Then, why you settin' here in this Jim Crow Car?"

"Why can't I sit here? I paid my fare."

"Let me edjicate you a little, Miss. You see, the rule is that when we get to your Capitol, that's Washington DC, we have to sit in these separate cars. So to avoid the trouble, we Jim Crow ourselves here in New York."

"I still don't understand," Betty responded in confusion.

"Jim Crow, that's the way the Man segregates the races. Do you get it now?" she explained defiantly.

Betty really knew about Jim Crow, but wanted to hear it from the other woman. She felt so ashamed. After a while the two women became friendly and talked and shared food that they brought or purchased at the stops and soon fell asleep. As the countryside passed in review, Betty saw what she had only read about. She saw the shanties, the poorly worked farms and some of the elegant homes as well. Yes, she was being educated.

Bart met her and they clung to one another. He carried her suitcase and they walked the few blocks to the house where she would stay. It was a Thursday and he had obtained a weekend pass, and they would go to a local spot called White Lake and spend the weekend there. Bart had borrowed a car and they left, happy and free for their vacation.

/ / / / / / / / / / / / / / /

Chapter Thirty-Nine
White Lake

It was an idyllic spot with overhanging weeping willow trees and other lush greenery. They were happy and very much in love. They made love almost in desperation, as if this might be the last time. Bart told her of his plan to speak to the Red Cross about his Mom and her need for frequent injections. His other siblings were unavailable. His brother had avoided the draft, was married, and lived in Florida. His sister had married a doctor, who was overseas, and she had become pregnant just before he left. She lived on Long Island. At the end of their holiday, they reluctantly returned to Fayetteville. Bart arose early to get to the camp and participate in the training.

The next morning, Betty decided to walk into town and look around. She was looking at the stores and was surprised to see a small luncheonette called the Brooklyn Diner. She started to laugh at the incongruity of the name and was looking at the window when she bumped into somebody and started to apologize. It was a black elderly man.

"Please, Ma'am, continue your walkin'."

"But it was my fault and I'm sorry," Betty replied.

"No ma'am, just go away," and with that he stepped off the sidewalk and ran away.

Once again, Betty was nonplussed by this incident and told Bart when he came in the evening.

"Oh, you silly fool, do you know what would have happened if anybody had seen that interchange?

"But I was at fault, I was trying to apologize."

"Yeah, but this is the South," Bart answered. "He would have been accused of molesting a white woman and would have been arrested. You've read about lynching. Well, they still happen. Be careful, honey."

She certainly learned her lesson. She never forgot and she repeated this story many, many times in her later years.

When she returned home to New York City, she soon received mail with unbelievable news. Bart had been successful in reaching the Red Cross. They had gone to see Bella, confirmed her diagnosis, and with the Commanding Officer's (CO's) permission, Bart's request for a transfer was granted and he was transferred to Fort Jay on Governor's Island in New York City.

/ / / / / / / / / / / / / / /

Chapter Forty
Weather Station

One day, while at Governor's Island, Bart noticed an ad for meteorologists. Betty had completed her work at school and was now eligible for such a position. She applied and landed the job.

She went to work at the weather station at Fort Monmouth in New Jersey. They were separated again, but soon resolved that dilemma. They rented a room in Elizabeth, New Jersey, which was halfway between their two locations. It was a short commute and they felt it was their first home. They had a small kitchen, so they could eat breakfast and dinner together. They bought a radio/phonograph, which still exists today - seventy years later!

The meteorological (weather) station was a research and development site and did not have a public face (It did not announce any weather information). However, it was conducted as a regular weather station. In those days there were no computers or satellites to receive and analyze conditions. Teletype information was received from stations from Chicago eastward. With this information received from stations located in cities or airports east of Chicago, plus data accumulated on site, maps were configured. There was a flat roof above and a garage below.

Balloons of two types were inflated in the garage, and at a signal from the observer on the roof with a theodolyte, a surveyor type instrument could track the balloons in flight in a horizontal and vertical direction. One balloon had a metal box and a parachute suspended from it. This instrument was called a radiosonde and contained a transmitter and devices to record atmospheric pressure, air temperature and humidity. The second balloon was called a PIBAL or pilot balloon to determine wind direction aloft.

At a given signal the radiosonde balloon was released and the tracker would record the position every minute or so and the recorder would record the information. When the pressure inside the balloon was greater than the upper atmosphere pressure, it would burst and the parachute would bring it back to land. Stamped on the outside of the radiosonde was the following: THIS IS US GOV'T PROPERTY PLEASE RETURN TO THE NEAREST GOVERNMENT AGENCY.

The station received a call from an excited farmer one day, who said he found this box. We invited him to return it to us quickly. Soon, this man in blue overalls arrived in his pickup and was beaming with pride. The Colonel, who was the commanding officer of the station, came down to thank this man.

"And where is our box?" the colonel said.

"Oh, I protected it real well," the farmer replied.

"And how did you do that?"

"Well, if you look in the back of my truck, you'll see that I immediately put it into a bucket of water, for safety."

The entire staff assembled for this event just couldn't contain their laughter so they ran upstairs to get a camera to record this patriotic scene. Of course, as the case was fitted with electronic equipment, it was all lost. But all present made this farmer very happy.

Betty spent a very happy year at the station, made several

friends but was happy to move on. Bart, once again had some good news. He had obtained housing at Fort. Jay on Governor's Island and they could move in shortly. But before they moved, they had to deal with a question that disturbed Bart.

On one of their last weekends in Elizabeth, they took the train to Asbury Park, which was a lovely seaside resort with a wide boardwalk flanked by many stores and games and other recreational activities. It was famous for the straw vehicles, which could seat three people and the attendants would push these carts up and down the boardwalk. It was a lovely way to enjoy the view of the ocean and watch the people, some dressed in Sunday finery.

Betty and Bart (B&B) sat on a bench facing the sea when Bart said, "We have to talk about something very important. We now have a home, and hopefully, I will not go overseas. I am now a sergeant with increased pay, and you will soon get another job. I think we should begin to think about saving for the future."

Betty concurred.

"However," he continued, "You have to tell your mother to go to work."

Betty reacted with conflicting emotions. She knew Bart was right but, how was she to tell that to Stella? She knew Stella was capable of more than just cooking and cleaning. In fact, she had joined the American Women's Voluntary Services (AWVS) and was a very successful speaker at many venues, urging people to buy War Bonds.

"I will do what I can to contact some of my old buddies and see if we can find your Mom a job. Why don't you go home next week

164

and talk to your Mom? We will then have your salary and mine to begin to build our nest egg," Bart indicated with confidence.

/ / / / / / / / / / / / / / / /

Chapter Forty-One
Hospital/Emilia

Life continued fairly evenly for many months. Martin was happy with his seeming success as Director of Sales. He had settled into a routine and despite his occasional feelings of isolation and loneliness, he made no real effort to look for female companionship. His boss, Hansen, had tried to arrange a foursome with Martin, introducing him to some female friends of John's wife. But none of these dates seemed to interest him. He often wondered why. And deep down in his hidden thoughts were tender memories of his children and Stella. He rarely felt the temptation to reach back into the past. He always dismissed the thoughts reassuring himself that he was the victim, and he had turned his life around by himself. He felt proud and confident. Martin became more successful with the company. The company looked upon him as an effective portrayer of the good will his employer wanted to display. This feature, as well as his uncanny ability to communicate, made him a welcome addition to the short list of speakers at conventions promoting the company's products.

At one point, he was attending such a convention up north in San Francisco. Several of his colleagues and salesmen from other companies were at dinner. Martin had to participate in the drinking of liquor. He tried to limit his intake to wines, which had a lower alcoholic content. However, several of the guests pressured him to try some of their products. Martin was often very sloppy in the administering of his insulin. There were no home-use glucose meters, so that the patient could adjust the dosage as the blood sugar showed an increase. He began to feel dizzy and one of his colleagues asked him, if he was all right. He was just about to say, "I'm okay," when he blanched, slid off the chair and fell to the floor. He was unconscious and was rushed to the nearest hospital and placed on life support in the intensive care unit (ICU).

He was diagnosed as suffering from a high blood-sugar count, which had resulted in a diabetic coma. He recovered slowly and was transferred to a regular room. When he was able to walk around, he returned to the ICU to personally thank the staff for keeping him alive. One nurse seemed particularly concerned about his future care. He vaguely remembered her voice when she had cared for him. He shook her hand and asked her name.

She said, "I am Emilia Browning. I am so glad to see you looking well. You had a difficult time. You must be very vigilant in the future and come in to the hospital
frequently to have your blood sugar tested, so that your insulin intake can be monitored."

He felt so grateful for her concern.

He said, "Would you come to dinner with me when I get out, so that I can express my thanks for your interest?"

She was surprised at this offer as no patient had ever suggested such a thank you.

"I'd be delighted," she said and she quickly left.

Martin took a short leave from work to recuperate and decided to stay in San Francisco. He liked the city and became interested in seeing Emilia, which he continued to do. Something was disturbing him, and he wasn't sure what it was. He was staying at the hotel, where the conference was held. He recalled an incident that dredged up past memories. Among some of the participants at the conference was a man whom he seemed to remember from the past. He couldn't pull up his name, but sitting in his room and thoughtful, he jumped out of the chair and shouted to no one, "He is Sam Sundberg, a friend of Joe!" He wasn't too happy at this revelation and tried to put it out of his mind, but it hung there, a dark cloud on his relatively comfortable existence.

His relationship with Emilia deepened, and he felt very close to her. He maintained the same false front with no family connections back in the East, to which, he hoped never to return. They both felt a closeness and caring for one another. She had never been married and expected to remain that way. She had come west from a small farming town in Nebraska. Her parents were gone but a married brother still ran the family farm. Martin was in a quandary. He wanted to be honest with Emmy, but was not sure how much of his hidden past life to reveal. He struggled with the problem for many weeks and despite the growing intimacy, he was reluctant to open up to the whole history. He reasoned that he had lived for many years, successfully, among people of diverse backgrounds and interests and no one seemed to want to dig any deeper into his life than what he was willing to divulge. He was satisfied with his own distorted attitude that he was protecting everyone by his continued silence on the question of his marriage, his children, and the wretched life he had left so many years ago.

Several weeks passed and he felt well enough to return to work. He was sorry to leave San Francisco, but Emilia and he planned to see one another on weekends. Work was steadily improving, and he really enjoyed his life, especially with Emilia. Rarely did thoughts of Stella and the children disturb his euphoria, until, one day, upon returning to the office, he saw a note: *Mr. Danzig called. Call him back!*

The phone call message presaged the pinprick in the bubble. Sam Sundberg had recognized Martin at the conference, but not his new persona as a talented member of a corporation. Sundberg did not approach Martin, but saved his gossip for where it would yield the most benefit. He returned to his home base in Kansas City, which was Scharlin's home base as well. Sam gave Scharlin the information and if it proved useful, the payment would be substantial. Scharlin called Joe. When the call was finished, he sat pensively for a few minutes and thoughts of Joe crept into his mind.

Joe's family was content. Lucy had married well and lived in DC. Janette, Evie's older sister, had two children who attended college in North Carolina and settled there. The youngest was still at loose ends. Joe's younger son was not a happy camper. Joe wanted him in the business, but his interests were more mundane. He wanted to be an auto mechanic!

Joe was horrified. He and Evie were now patrons of the Arts and were seen in the newspapers walking down the aisle at the Met Opera with Lawrence Tibbett, a favorite opera star at the time.

To avoid any embarrassment, Joe bought a garage for his son in California. It was a disaster. His son was not a business man and the garage was lost. He returned to work for Joe, a very unhappy man to this day.

Joe and Evie built a home in Rockland County, which was 'country,' but along with Janette and the Larkins, it became an enclave called The Birches. This land, which Joe purchased sometime in the late 1930's, turned out to be a windfall purchase. In later years most of the open land he owned was needed by the Thruway Authority for right of way purposes and he sold the property at enormous profit. All soon gave up their city homes and relocated to the country houses permanently. However, the Danzig's also had a pied a terre in lower Manhattan near the department store, "Wanamaker's". Evie had a second grand piano in the apartment to continue her love of music. They were very successful people who did not want anything to interfere with their elitist status.

Joe continued to accumulate wealth and some of it by his connections with borderline criminal elements. They were used to assist him in securing funds and ease of operation through the governmental quagmire. This collusion between business empires and the gray area of graft and fraud with government agencies was rampant then. Scandals abounded and corporate's nefarious activities were unfettered by regulations and legislative overlook. Of course, when Martin was a part of this "inner circle," he was privy to all of this underground activity. Eventually, in the 1950's, charges were leveled and Joe went to a "Banker's Jail," which meant he appeared every day, checked in and left to continue his life without interruption.

When Joe heard from Scharlin about Sam's encounter with Martin, he did not know, how much of Joe's activities Martin had revealed to anyone in the industry. He had to develop some way to keep Martin quiet. He decided to use Evie.

Evie and Joe made a trip to California, so that Evie could reassure herself that Martin was well. Joe then used his well honed skill to elicit from Martin what, if anything, he had revealed of Joe's operation. Joe's bargaining chip was the promise that information of Martin's past life would never be revealed. In return, Martin would not reveal Joe's past business operations in New York.

Joe was determined to keep a closer eye on Martin. Joe continued to urge Martin to move east and promised him a more lucrative position. It was 1970 and Martin had been promoted to District Manager in northern California. Emilia joined Martin in his apartment but they did not marry, although she was called Mrs. Lang. Joe needed some inducements to convince Martin to return to New York. He urged Evie to call Martin, establish a closer tie with Emmy and urge him to consider relocating. Evie was planning some kind of a family event with their children and Janette's which she hinted would be an easy way for Martin to re-enter the family and introduce Emilia.

Martin and Emilia were planning a trip to Europe and would stop to visit with the family. In a call that Martin made to Evie, Martin asked to speak to Joe and told Joe that Sam had called Martin to tell him of a more lucrative position in New York. Martin asked Joe to intercede and forward the information. Joe was delighted. This was just what he had hoped. He now would not appear as a promoter, but as a supporter.

Martin and Emmy did get to Europe, a first for both and they eagerly traveled from one major city to another, thoroughly enjoying

171

their adventures together. They returned on the Statendam and stopped at a hotel in New York. Nostalgia and quiet pain enveloped him in memory of his teenage years as a young boy husband and father. He dismissed the thoughts quickly as he had learned to do these many years of his wanderlust. He phoned Joe and inquired about Sam's proposal. Joe said that nothing had been decided, but to keep the idea alive, because there might be news soon. With that information, Martin and Emmie took the train and returned to California.

/ / / / / / / / / / / / / /

Chapter Forty-Two
Governor's Island

Governor's Island was an unusual location. It was a very green, well-preserved island in the bay at the entrance to the famous harbor of New York City. A ten minute ferry ride would bring you to South Ferry in lower Manhattan, just a short walk to the subway that would take you almost anywhere within the city limits. Of course, Staten Island, which was beyond Governor's Island at that time, could only be reached by ferry.

Betty and Bart enjoyed setting up house with some furniture provided by the army, and some of the accoutrements donated by their mothers. The island had been an active fort with fortifications preserved from both the Revolutionary and Civil Wars. It housed a prison which was used during the Second World War. It had some gentle hills and at the crest of one stood the mansion which was the home of General Hugh Drum. There was a huge open green space which was used for parades and other military activities. At the edge of the grounds was the hospital, where Bart worked as the manager of the radiology department with Major Ed Wuphrat, the doctor in charge. The non-com quarters were beyond the parade grounds. The hierarchal structure of the army would not even 'think' of placing non-commissioned officers in close proximity to the commissioned ones.

One day as Betty was in the PX (store for groceries, clothing, etc.) making a few purchases and was walking out of the PX, Mrs.

Drum said, "Good morning." Betty, surprised at the greeting, responded in kind and proceeded to walk across the quadrangle towards the area where non-com soldiers lived. She could hear the comment Mrs. Drum made as she left her presence, with a "Hhu, the nerve to talk to me in that 'friendly manner'." She never acknowledged Betty after that and Betty did likewise. The caste system at work!

At the far end of the island was a fertile area which was soon converted into victory gardens and each family was given a plot to grow vegetables. Betty and Bart had great fun seeing the food grow and using it.

In addition to the staff which administered the facility, there were prisoners who had been taken during the campaign from North Africa up the boot of Italy pushing Mussolini's steel-booted Fascist Army northward. These prisoners were shipped to the states and some were housed in the prison at Ft. Jay. They were permitted to work on the island. They were very pleasant young men who assisted the families by clearing the grounds, collecting trash and garbage. Of course, as this was the 40's, there still were ethnic and racial slurs imposed on anyone who didn't fit the concept of what was an American. The term that was used to allude to the prisoners was *Come te que llama?* (which roughly translated as, *What is your name?*).

B&B soon settled into a routine, and it was time for Betty to go back to work. Once again, Bart was adept at filtering out employment opportunities for Betty. This time he found an ad for engineers to work on some war-time materiel development.

Although Betty was not trained as an engineer, Bart convinced her to try, saying, "You are a quick study; it will not be a problem."

/ / / / / / / / / / / / / /

Chapter Forty-Three
ITT?

With her resume in hand and with Bart's confidence, if not much of her own, she went to the offices of International Telephone and Telegraph, and applied for the job. A Mr. Pickels conducted the interview and he said in a sort of non -believing way,

"I don't understand why you are applying for this position. Your background is not very relevant to our needs."

"But my husband said that I am a quick learner." They both laughed at this non sequitur.

"Well, what can you tell me from your geoscience background?" Mr. Pickels asked.

"I know a good deal about rivers," Betty responded.

"Hmm, OK, I'll give you ten minutes and when I return I want you to tell me all about rivers. Is that agreeable?" asked Mr. Pickels.

Betty was ecstatic. She had written a paper on the Hudson River and had walked and photographed a good portion of the river on the lower banks of the river. She was hired and placed in the shop to learn about the structure of the mobile radar units that were being developed at the site for use in the Pacific Theater of the War.

She became quite proficient in the cutting of the chassis, the soldering of electrical connections and the wiring within the units which resembled the old style telephone booths. She then was upgraded to Instrumentation and then finally to assisting the engineers.

At home, there was always the constant anxiety of who would

be the next to go overseas to fight. Bart's name never appeared. Betty left work when she became pregnant. Even though the times were so precarious, they wanted a child while they were still young. Kara was born, accepted with joy from every quarter.

Betty's brother, Henry, was seeing a lovely girl, Bonnie. They came over for dinner Christmas night and as they left late, B&B got to bed later than usual. Within an hour she was disturbed, and Bart called for an ambulance. They had to go off the Island as the island hospital was filled with returning soldiers, and there was no room for staff wives. It was a strange trip, up to the Bronx Lebanon Hospital, at that point, considered Army property. The ambulance backed into a driveway, and the attendants were about to pull the litter out, when two soldiers in white said,

"Darn, another stiff, at this hour."

Hearing that, Betty sat up and Bart yelled, "Where the hell are we?"

"Oh, gee, I'm sorry, but you have come to the morgue!" the soldiers said.

The ambulance backed out of the driveway and went to the proper entrance. As Betty still was not ready for delivery, Bart was urged to go home and get some rest. The next morning at 6:00am Kara was born, December 26, 1944.

Henry was drafted soon after Kara's birth, despite a rather serious infection on his leg, which he had received while handling animal skins from South America. These skins were imported by the company where he had been employed. When he had been examined at the induction station, the infection seemed to have subsided.

177

However, within less than a year he was discharged due to the weakness of the infected leg. Bonnie visited him in St. Louis where he was stationed. He was prepared to give her a ring in anticipation of an engagement and eventual marriage.

His world went topsy-turvy when in St. Louis, she refused. Her explanation to Stella, who was very disappointed also, was that Bonnie felt that Henry was too money and business directed, and this was not her interest. In addition, she felt that he had a roaming eye, and, although she cared for him, she felt that marriage was too important a step to start with such misgivings.

In later years, when both were married to other people, they renewed a friendship with their respective families. He, upon return to civilian life, went seeking new women and found one very quickly. Within a very short time he married Lynda, who was a very attractive woman deeply in love with Henry. Although Henry loved Lynda, it was not the way he had loved Bonnie. Bart and Betty felt that Henry still had lingering feelings about Bonnie.

Lynda was a sweet good natured woman. She did not have the depth of perception of values or a worldly outlook, which Henry had so loved about Bonnie. Lynda was more concerned with superficiality. Appearances and gossipy stories seemed her métier. She wore her clothes well and looked elegant and Henry enjoyed the stares and comments of friends. Today we would call her arm candy. She was a good wife and a devoted mother. Henry was grateful for that. Bart and Betty were amused by her minimal interests and wondered how long Henry would last in the marriage.

/ / / / / / / / / / / / / / /

Chapter Forty-Four

Benjamin

Stella had never had the young adolescent experience of working outside of the home. She was pregnant at fifteen and a mother and wife with responsibilities at sixteen. When Betty suggested that Stella go to work, it was an emotional shock to her entire system. However, Bart kept his promise and arranged for her to work in a small lace factory, which was a union shop.

She developed friendships with other women and learned about the theater and places to dine. She became a much happier person. Her appearance changed and her style of dress changed. She liked who she was.

One day, one of the women asked about her husband. Up to this point she had retained espousing the myth that he still represented a factor in her life. She always felt that this gave her a sense of identity and a fear of exposing herself to the painful truth. She met several divorced women, who did not consider this a badge of dishonor. In fact, they felt better about themselves, in that they had removed themselves from a bad marriage. Stella finally broke her silence and told her friends the truth. She felt as if a burden had been removed from her shoulders.

"But you are still married to him. Why?"

The women suggested that she get a lawyer and find a way to free herself completely. She discovered that there was a law in New York State called, The Enoch Arden Law, which stated that if a spouse had not supported you for at least seven years and had not shared your bed for that time, you could receive a decree, which was essentially a divorce. She told Betty and Henry of her decision, and they were delighted with the news. She removed her marriage ring and felt like a young girl again. She was in her early forties. Her only sadness was the lingering feeling of loss of her first and, she felt, only love, but it was soon tempered with the anger and distaste and resentment and almost hate she felt by Martin's abandonment.

/ / / / / / / / / / / / / / /

Chapter Forty-Five
Telephone Call

He, Martin, however, felt nothing. He had inured himself to forgetting and lived in the present only. The only obstacle to this self-imposed philosophy was the persistent, albeit, much diminished now, sweet memories of Betty, and he often wondered if he would recognize her if he met her in the street.

When Martin and Emilia returned from New York after their trip to Europe, they settled into their routines at their respective jobs. Emilia continued to work at the hospital in the Cardiac Intensive Care Unit. She loved her work and was an efficient nurse. Some of her co-workers prodded her with questions about her personal life. They could not understand why she didn't have a marriage ring. At that point in time, the 50's, it was an uncommon situation for two people to live together without the benefit of marriage. It bothered her as well. Martin did not discuss this with her very often, but he explained that they had no intention of having children, so a marriage was not an urgency. She did not understand his reasoning fearing that he was hiding something from her, but she loved him and trusted him, so she accepted the situation as he wished.

Evie, Joseph's wife, continued to call them at fairly frequent intervals, but at one call several months after their return, it was Joe who called.

"Well, it is all set. You can plan to return to New York whenever you can close up your business there. You will still work for the same company in the same capacity, but your region will be Westchester. We will begin to look for a home for you somewhere near the bridge, so that you will easily travel across it to our home in Rockland County," Joe elaborated.

Martin was just a bit uneasy about returning to New York because of the proximity to Stella and family. Emilia was disturbed by the role that Joe was playing and Martin was accepting. She did not like his manipulating of their lives. She felt he was doing it with impunity, without even the courtesy of involving them in these important decisions. The only time she had been within the family group, she noticed Joe's manner. He rarely listened to Evie, or any one else. It was his way or no way. She knew he was a successful man, but she always felt he was a very insecure one. She was not very fond of him, but if Martin felt it was OK, she had to accept that as well.

Very soon, thereafter, they received the call from Joe, who said he had put a binder on a lovely house in Tarrytown, a beautiful, historic town where Washington Irving had created the famous character of Rip Van Winkle. The house was located near the bridge to Rockland County as Joe had indicated. They then began the preparation to relocate. They began the work of ending their commitments in San Francisco and made preparation to move. They would ship their household goods and personal effects to be transported by truck. Evie said she would be happy to go to the Tarrytown house and receive the household effects.

They sent their household goods before they left, as they wanted to drive east and stop for a few days to visit her brother, Jim, at the farm. Martin had his job waiting for him, but Emilia was still writing to the local hospitals to find work for herself. Martin tried to convince her not to seek employment, but she was insistent in wanting to work.

Martin still had some anxiety about the relocation, because he was concerned about the proximity for the exposure to public view of his past. However, it was curious that the feelings were not of his role in this debacle. This ability to live such a duplicitous life raises many questions of major psychological and personality defects. To block out the first thirty-five years of one's life, negate the existence of those involved, seems to indicate some serious implications. Despite the above, he undertook the beginning of the next phase of his odyssey.

The trip was uneventful with Emilia more interested in the scenery as they crossed the Rockies onto the Plains. The vast topographical differences in the country became so evident. Crossing the farmland, she noted how vast the "breadbasket" of the country was. Corn and wheat crops covered miles of fertile land. As this was now in the 50's, the country had begun to recover from the strain of the war and productivity was increasing both in agriculture and industry. The manufacturing of household consumer goods was growing and men returning from the war were anxious to return to peacetime pursuits.

Of course, there were many veterans who were faced with injuries and lack of skills needed in this post war period. The trade unions had revived their role and had become the spearhead, with students and other organizations representing young people, women and other oppressed groups, into a people's coalition that by sheer numbers was able to effect changes. Fortunately, there was a president who was receptive to the demands for assistance. Legislation was introduced and passed by Congress to establish the many safety nets we now accept as ordinary and natural. Among these were the GI Bill which afforded veterans health care and training for jobs. Social Security provided the aging population a means of survival. Unemployment insurance gave the unemployed a leg up between jobs. For those of us who remember the times without these laws, the attempt to reduce and destroy these life preservers now is criminal!

As the eastward-bound couple began to approach Chicago and Detroit, the industrial heart of the country was full of activity. There seemed to be a lightness in the air. Clothes looked different. People looked relieved of the anxiety of loss of family due to the war. Many changes were happening in Europe and the Far East. Some of these changes were due to the increased knowledge in technology as a result of the war. In some instances, the US began to see trade benefits with some of these outlying countries.

/ / / / / / / / / / / / / / /

Chapter Forty-Six

Discharged

By this time, the war in Europe was over and in the Pacific Theater as well. There was much excitement in New York and especially at Fort Jay. Discharges for the servicemen had been based on the accumulation of points. Soldiers who saw service in combat had the adequate numbers to be discharged. For stateside soldiers, it was a little more difficult. However, Bart had what was called mattress points, a child, which gave him the points needed to qualify for discharge. The hospital tried to convince him to sign up with the peacetime army, because then he would have a job guaranteed.

B&B laughed at this suggestion as they couldn't wait to return to civilian life and some sense of normalcy. They had adjusted to army life and had befriended many of the drafted and regular army families. Their living quarters became the center where many of the soldiers who had come from western states found living in a big city very intimidating. These young soldiers preferred staying on the post and mostly hanging out in B&B's living room. One of the soldiers was an easterner and did not seem to fit the mold of the other young draftees. He seemed older than most of the other GI's. He cozied up to Bart, who was the senior man of the group. He said that he owned a bar and café near Cape Cod, and invited Bart and Betty to come and visit when discharged.

There were economic, housing and employment problems facing all the returning veterans. Bart was fortunate that he never had to deal with combat. With the aftermath of several wars in which the

US was involved in subsequent years, the physiological and psychological impact on returning vets was soon classified as post traumatic distress syndrome. Although this syndrome did not have a name immediately after World War II, the condition was rampant, misunderstood, and allowed to fester. Many vets found it difficult to adjust to life after experiencing so much death of friends and comrades.

Bart's mother owned a two family house and provided one apartment for B&B. This was in Brooklyn, and it was a very convenient arrangement. At first, it was easy and comfortable. Bart found work in a hospital and continued his volunteer work as before. Betty was a stay-at-home mom for a while. Kara was a bright frolicsome child, now four years old and quite precocious. They decided to have another child.

Peter was born in 1949. Although it had been a normal pregnancy the birth was not. The baby was oxygen deprived and was retained in the nursery with intensive care nursing. The family knew of the child's difficulty, but the information was kept from Betty. When a nurse casually mentioned the difficulty with Peter, Betty became frantic and demanded to see her baby. There was great concern for the entire family. After a week, they took him home and then began the life-long struggle to keep this child well and alive.

The following year, Betty went to enroll Kara in kindergarten, but discovered that the school did not have one. With Betty's permission, they placed Kara in first grade, because she knew how to read. One day while practicing penmanship, Kara wrote with her left hand. The principal came in and a short battle ensued. When the principal put the pencil in Kara's right hand, Kara promptly returned it to her left. After several exchanges, the principal announced, imperiously,

"This child must learn to write correctly, that means in the right hand!"

When Kara explained the incident to Betty, her response was, "You must do whatever the teacher says. That is the rule." It was 1950 - no parental input yet...

Betty now faced with a sick child, just gave up her thought of ever being able to go back to work. She was so distraught not knowing what was really wrong with her baby. Also, not wanting to spend all her time with the illness, which might detract from her responsibility towards Kara and Bart, it was a very difficult time. A friend, Blanche, was taking her daughter to an office where children with cerebral palsy were treated. She suggested that Betty take Peter there.

The doctor said, "You do not belong here, but tell me about your son."

Betty then related all the conditions she noticed that the child endured, including convulsions, difficulty in breathing, eating. The doctor then called another doctor, and an appointment was made to see a researcher of neurological diseases. Peter's condition was called a dysfunction of the autonomic nervous system.

The most disturbing news was when the neurologist said, "I regret to tell you that he probably will not survive beyond five to six years."

Burdened with this devastating news, which B&B never

relayed to family, life became a profound struggle for survival. Bart and Betty faced with the possible loss of their child decided to become pregnant again.

When Betty went for a checkup, the physician said, "No more babies for you. You have a tumor in your uterus which must come out. It is pre-cancerous."

Betty was despondent. After the surgery, she went into a deep depression with thoughts of suicide. With Bart's close attention and time, she recovered.

Both grandmothers were kind and generous doing what they could to reduce the strain of caring for a sick child. They were convenient baby sitters. However, as Bella's hearing was impaired, they would leave the children in her care only if B&B would return in the late evening. Stella was certainly younger and physically fit. B & B wanted to go to Europe.

Henry was now a successful entrepreneur with a trucking company in lower Manhattan. One of his customers was the Holland Bulb Company, which shipped the flower bulbs to New York via the Holland American Shipping Line, where his trucks would pick up the cargo and truck it all across the US. Henry suggested that B&B take a ship and visit some customers in Europe. And that is what they did. They sailed on the Statendam with great fanfare, as was the custom in the 50-60's. They were so excited by this unbelievable adventure, as well as it being a way to heal some of the sadness concerning Pete's illness. And what an adventure it was and how it opened their eyes to the world.

Chapter Forty-Seven
Life at Work

Stella was feeling almost euphoric, with what she considered her good fortune. Her children were married with children of their own. She earned enough to support herself and dress fashionably. Of course, Peter was a sadness, and it hurt her. She enjoyed her work and her friendships with several women. If she thought of Martin, at all, she never revealed her feelings of loss and abandonment.

Gertrude, one of the women in the office, remarked, "You look pretty snazzy today, Stella. Going to meet your boyfriend?"

Stella laughed, "Yeah, sure, they're lining up downstairs and I have my choice, Edmund Lowe or Rudy Vallee!"

"No, I'm not kidding. You are young and really pretty. Why don't you think about a man friend now that you received your divorce?" Gertrude said.

"Well, I'm a grandma now. I think I'll pass," Stella said.

"You are wrong, but suit yourself," Gertrude countered.

This interchange set her to thinking of a subject about which she never allowed herself to ruminate. Well, she thought to herself, we'll see. She just didn't feel that she should consciously pursue it.

It was a Friday and she always liked to wander into Macy's on a Friday afternoon. She felt relaxed as she had no special chores to perform, and she needed to pick up a pair of shoes, which she had ordered. She felt very much a sophisticated New Yorker with her Macy's credit card and a new checking account. She wandered about the store, purchased some cosmetics and then picked up her shoes.

It was just past 6 o'clock, and she had the urge for a cup of coffee. She thought for a moment and then, with a smile on her face, said out loud to nobody in particular,

"I am going to have dinner in a restaurant."

She always thought eating out was an unnecessary and extravagant indulgence, but today it seemed like the right thing to do. She had never had the experience of the life of a working woman. She realized all that she had missed as a teenage mother. She had never been in a position to explore the city on her own. She had always been protected by family. This sheltering shield was now being shattered and unbelievable light and experience began to filter into her life. One of the many exciting new phenomena was the ability to have money in hand that she secured by herself with no pleading or begging and buy a few things which she either needed or wanted. She still retained her modest thriftiness which she had of necessity acquired when she had lived on money doled out to her out of pity.

Across the street was a Horn and Hardhart Automat, today no longer there, which always had excellent coffee. She always thought it was fun to be able to pick what you wanted and have the little door magically open and there it was! She made her selection and looked for an empty table, but there was none visible. Suddenly, she saw a man waving to her. Not knowing the person, she inched forward.

He said, "You can sit here. I'm leaving soon."

"Oh, please don't leave on my account. I don't mind sharing the table," Stella noted.

"Thank you very much, I'll just finish my tea," the gentleman

190

said. "I see you also made some purchases at Macy's."

"Oh, do you work near here?" Stella asked.

"No, I work in the Wall Street area, but I like to buy my pajamas here," the man explained.

"Why doesn't your wife do that?" Stella questioned. "I always bought them for my husband." She knew she was treading on dangerous ground, so she carefully avoided calling herself a widow.

"Unfortunately, my wife died two years ago and I do the buying now," the man sadly replied.

"I am so sorry, I guess I...er am in the same situation," Stella hesitantly replied. "My husband is gone many years," she said as she looked at this quiet man with a gentle smile on his face.

She was careful not to say that he was dead. There seemed to be something immoral about saying someone was dead when he wasn't. Stella's last remark seemed to open the floodgates and conversation flowed. Mostly they spoke of family and children and the problems of living alone. They talked for almost an hour and drank several cups of coffee before Stella realized it was time to leave.

"Where do you live?" was the question each asked the other.

When they both indicated Brooklyn, there was unrestrained laughter and he took her hand in grateful appreciation of their commonality. He took her home and they planned future meetings.

For Stella, memories of handsome Martin lingered mixed with the anger and thoughts of the deprivation he had caused. The man she had met, Benjamin, she saw as a caring person with a secure position. He was an accountant and worked for the Workman's Compensation Board. He was involved with worker-employer investigations of legal violations.

She soon felt emotionally tied to this man, and they thought of marriage. Stella was determined to make a new life for herself. Benjamin's three children took to Stella quickly and easily and Stella took care to always be caring and warm towards his children and their families.

Betty and Henry were now on the back burner, as her focus was Benjamin and his family. This arrangement suited both families very well. Betty and Henry were so delighted with Stella's new existence. It made them proud and secure in the knowledge that Stella was no longer alone and struggling. She had prepared them for the radical change her marriage created. Her focus was Benjamin and his family, which suited them both very well as Benjamin's family did not interest Betty and Henry at all. Stella and Benjamin seemed self-absorbed and were not inclined to include Betty and Henry–all to the good, Betty and Henry, laughingly remarked privately.

/ / / / / / / / / / / / / / /

Chapter Forty-Eight
Young Peter

It soon became apparent to Betty and Bart realizing that they were facing a major health problem with their young son. His life expectancy was limited and their hopes of having another child were soon shattered when major surgery made Betty no longer able to have a child. Their lives revolved around Peter and the struggle and anxiety accompanying the goal of keeping the young boy alive. Betty felt that she was locked into a corral with high fences and no chance of escape.

In the late 50s, Bart's mother died and they saw the opportunity to move elsewhere. It became a paramount concern, as the demography of the community had shifted and they saw a need to find a new home. Kara was eleven and Pete was six. Finding new schools for them became easier at this point. With Henry's assistance, they were able to relocate to an old Tudor house, not far from Henry and Lynda's home. Though Betty and Bart were now geographically close to Henry and Lynda, they were astronomically years apart in attitude.

One day, Betty was walking Peter to school (he had difficulty walking so Betty took him in a stroller and left the carriage well before reaching the schoolyard). A woman, seeing this, approached and asked if there was anything she could do to help. Her son was in the same class as Peter. This class was considered a special one for students with special skills. As Peter was adept in mathematical concepts, he was a natural for this placement. Leon was a good musician and that was his specialty. This class also was part of the orchestra preparation group. Leon played the saxophone. It was difficult to select an instrument for Peter, as his coordination was not exemplary. Although he played the piano, there already were two assigned pianists. The teacher, Mr. Gee, finally selected the glockenspiel.

As they were required to take the instruments home over the weekend, it was difficult for Peter to carry it. Another student, Garry, a husky young man, suggested that he carry the item home for Peter and in return, Peter agreed to tutor Garry in math. This friendship developed and lasted until Peter's death at age thirty in June 1980.

Betty and the woman, Barbara, soon became friends, and Betty indicated her frustration in dealing with a sick child. Barbara suggested that Betty join the Parents Association and maybe help run a club after school. She offered to take Peter to her house on that day. This worked out well and Betty soon had students produce a newspaper from the Journalism Club, which Betty had established.

Somehow this wasn't enough. Barbara noted that Betty did well with children and should maybe teach. Betty passed the teaching exam and began a new chapter in her life as a teacher of the Earth Sciences in secondary schools.

/ / / / / / / / / / / / / /

Chapter Forty-Nine
Westchester

After Martin and Emilia returned from Europe, they received the call from Joseph indicating the purchase of a home in Tarrytown. As this would be a splendid time for a short holiday, they decided to drive across the country to their new home. The nagging question of their relationship, that is the lack of a marriage, was of more concern to Emilia, but did not bother Martin that much. Instead, he was concerned with the proximity to his old life. He knew that New York was so big it was possible to get lost in it. He quickly banished all thoughts of the past and satisfied himself with plans for the future.

For Emilia and Martin, New York loomed on the horizon. The reality of relocation was their concern. When they approached the house which was to be their home, they were delighted and amazed at its location, surrounded by a mini forest and the beauty of its exterior and interior. They were overwhelmed. Emilia momentarily forgave Joseph, Martin's brother-law for his interference in their lives.

Joseph continued to maintain a close contact with the new residents. In fact Joseph made a great effort to involve Emilia with the life of the Danzigs and Wetzlars. This strengthening of the "familial bond" was insurance that Martin would be kept on the correct path and not be tempted to reveal any of the sordid actions of Joseph's business activity. Martin was happy that Emmy was close to his family. It took some of the pressure off him. He enjoyed the work and soon began to look for activities beyond the job. As they had a fairly sizeable property, they engaged a gardener. In discussions with Senor Giordano (or Gordie as they called him), they decided to build a greenhouse attached to a portion of the rear of the house. Here it would be possible for Martin to germinate plants and house them during the winter months. Martin soon became fascinated with the possibilities of growth of rare plants. He began to visit gardening shops and extensive greenhouses and learned a good deal about flowering plants that were native to the region. He also began to participate, once again, in the activities of the local Boy Scouts. There seemed to be a need for him to somehow connect to young boys. One wonders whether his aborted fatherhood of a boy child whom he did not see to grow up to an adolescent or a man, triggered this interest. In his quiet moments, his troubled mind often conjured up scenarios where he would accidentally meet his children. He realized that they were grown now, but Joseph never engaged in any discussion as to their whereabouts or with what they were involved.

Only once did Martin raise the question, and he was greeted with a curt response from Joseph: "I don't know and just don't bother me with that old history. I am not interested and neither should you be."

Martin recoiled from this answer but it did not shut his mind from dreaming.

One day at work, he was engaged in a conversation with a customer at the latter's office, when the phone rang and he apologized for taking the call, saying it was of vital personal importance. When he finished the call, the customer indicated that an elderly uncle of his wife's who had Alzheimer's had slipped out of the house and was missing for twelve hours. The family had engaged a detective agency to assist the police in attempting to locate him and they believed they had some definitive clues. Somehow that information resonated with Martin. He knew he could not reveal his intentions to anyone. He decided to travel to another town and speak to a detective agency. He drove to Chappaqua, a rather affluent community somewhat north of his location. This was not a good choice, so he went south to White Plains, a more commercial city. There he found several agencies, as there were many lawyers and courts in the town. Tom Sullivan seemed like a good choice. He was a seasoned operator and understood the need for secrecy. All Martin wanted was a brief description of Henry and his life. He knew that finding Betty would be more difficult, as she was probably married and perhaps living elsewhere. He gave no address or phone and said he would make the contact with the agency. Within a month, he had the information, and he had many mixed feelings of joy, misery and regret for the lost years. Tom extended his inquiry and found that Betty also had two children. (He was unbelievably a grandfather of four grandkids.) How sad that he couldn't share this news with anyone. *So be it. I chose this path and with it I shall remain*, he convinced himself. He felt satisfied that in his curiously distorted mind, he was content with his life.

Emilia had found work easily at Westchester Hospital, and Martin and she lived a very quiet comfortable existence. They saw Martin's family from time to time and were accepted readily as part of the family. Most of the children were either away at college or had established homes elsewhere. As most of the children went to the University of North Carolina at Chapel Hill, the Wetzlars soon thought

197

of retiring to that area. So this little microcosm of a family felt they were in a bubble of safety from all manner of disturbances. They had no connection with Stella or her life. They felt so secure in their comfort zone of adequate finances, they could indulge in almost any wish or need that might arise.

All the children were successful and Martin's family suffered little intrusion of the "hard knocks" which other less fortunate families endured. Even the grandparents lived a very simple unfettered existence. If they ever thought about Martin's children and/or Stella, it was difficult to discern. They all were stoic and never revealed their feelings or thoughts. They were totally intimidated by Joseph and his "management" of the family. Pop, Martin's father, retired and for the balance of his life, he occupied his time with little projects in a basement workshop, he had built for himself. One of his favorite activities was to buy old books and re-cover them with tooled leather. Some of these books found their way into Betty's possession. She never quite knew how she came to have a series of these hand tooled copies of Shakespeare's plays. Unfortunately, they disappeared due to the frequent change of location during the years after Martin left. When Grandma Larkin died, Evie sent a small silver butterfly pin to Betty, saying Grandma wanted her to have it. She still has it and often wonders what the other cousins received as their inheritance.

When Emmy reached sixty, she decided to retire. She became interested in literacy and went to the local library and read stories and tutored some of the few foreign students who struggled with learning to read and speak English. She did not make friends easily and Martin was the mixer. They had a few friends but entertained rarely. They did not venture into Manhattan for theater or dining. They always seemed to go north or go to Rockland County or New Jersey. Emilia thought it was strange, but never questioned Martin in this regard. She, however, did get to the city for shopping. So their lives continued in this rather ordinary way. The only impediment seemed to be Martin's ubiquitous diabetes, which needed constant monitoring, as well as his sometimes troubling cardiac difficulty. As he carried more weight than was comfortable for his frame, the stress on his heart was always of concern. He was told to lessen his caloric intake, which he refused. His exercise regimen was also limited. So the specter of heart attack was always on the horizon. Emmy was constantly on the lookout for symptoms.

/ / / / / / / / / / / / / / /

Chapter Fifty

Peter

There is probably no more difficult experience for young parents than to maintain a constant vigil over a child's illness. Betty and Bart knew that Peter's life span was limited. This was a very difficult awareness to sustain. Some early neurological tests indicated that the child had problems with his breathing. He was subject to many respiratory infections. He would have frequent bouts of loss of muscle function as well as convulsive episodes. His ability to swallow was limited and had to be learned. Many of these disturbing symptoms became a way of life for the young parents. Their constant focus was on Peter. He soon developed into a bright sweet young child. A diagnosis was reached when he was two years old and the family was told that his survival was limited.

At this point there was no hope of his longevity beyond five years. As life would work it out, he survived into adulthood. In puberty, he developed a severe kypho- scoliosis which reduced his respiratory capacity and required a tracheotomy with subsequent reliance on a respirator to sleep. Peter graduated from a university, was an excellent mathematician, and lived a fairly normal life with many restrictions, such as a cane to assist his walking and a respirator to assist his breathing. He had friends who treated him in a special way, always kindly and never alluding to his stature (five feet), but always relying on his judgment and clear thinking. He worked as a statistician for the Department of Labor, Bureau of Labor Statistics and managed to get to and from Manhattan by bus and taxi.

Bart, during this time became very concerned about Peter and began to show the stress Pete's illness caused. He became very depressed and withdrew into thoughtful silence. One day at work, he suffered a cardiac attack, the first of three which eventually resulted in a triple bypass surgery, a new procedure at the time. This new wrinkle compounded the responsibility for Betty in terms of becoming a health care giver. This stressed her day to day concerns and strained the relationship between Bart and herself. Although they both felt still very much in love, the stresses began to show. Bart would become less communicative, and Betty just did not know how to deal with it.

If she expressed concern for his welfare, he brushed her concern off with, "I'm OK. Just let me be."

He was not OK. He began to take long bike rides on Sundays, always telling her of the new parts of Manhattan he visited. She never questioned his stories. Peter and his health still remained the center of their life. Somehow small cracks began to show in Bart's strong concern for Peter's well-being. This seemed to be exacerbated by Bart's surgery.

One evening, visiting Peter in the hospital after an emergency trip to resolve his loss of breath, Dr. Nash was also visiting.

As they left the Intensive Care Unit and were waiting for the elevator, Bart said in a rather macabre tone, "Peter will not make it this time, yes?"

Dr. Nash responded calmly and solemnly, "Oh, yes, he will, as he has done many times before."

Bart then began pounding Dr. Nash's chest with his closed

fists, screaming, "No, he won't make it. No, he won't!" and turned away in tears. At home, Bart cried, "I just can't go the hospital anymore and watch Peter's suffering."

Betty reassured him that she would go and he did not have to go. Of course, he realized that he would never let her go alone and he retreated into his thoughtful silent mode until the next crisis took place. Peter's illness became more difficult to manage, as his breathing became more difficult. In time the doctors decided that something drastic was needed medically to save his life and a tracheostomy was performed, and for the rest of his life, Peter was dependent upon a respirator. He needed it to sleep and inflate his lungs once during the day. He was able to continue working, which was such an important part of his quest for normalcy.

At this time Bart and Betty decided to invest in a second home to allow Peter an opportunity for a "vacation" as air travel seemed too risky in his current condition. This was a boon for the entire family. It provided a different venue and the weekend escapes were responsible for a resurgence of Bart and Betty's confidentiality as well as an outlet for Bart's need to do something physical and productive. Everyone was delighted with the beautiful space and environment which became an important part of their lives for several years.

/ / / / / / / / / / / / / / /

Chapter Fifty-One
Phone Call

One evening, during the 1970's, Bart blurted out, "Say, honey, do you ever think about your father?"

Betty was so shocked by the question that she had to catch her breath. The question stirred up the memories, which always were hidden, yet close to the surface. She had always thought of the possibilities. She never thought of recourse to police or missing person's advocates and she felt so isolated by her Dad's family that it seemed like a dead end to even attempt a trial run.

She finally hesitated a bit and answered, "I think about him all the time."

"Well, why don't you do something about it?"

"What can I do?"

"Call your dear Uncle Joseph," he said, sarcastically.

"Oh, I can't do that. He won't talk to me."

"Well, there is no harm in trying."

After some difficulty in reaching for a resolve, deep within herself, she phoned.

Joseph, stunned by Betty's call, reacted after a few seconds of silence until he finally found his voice and answered. Betty blurted out the question which had lingered in her thoughts for so many years,

"Can you tell me of my father's whereabouts?"

He did not answer the question, but instead said, "Why don't you and your brother drive up for dinner some evening and we will talk."

Henry was delighted. He just loved to rub shoulders with the rich. He really did not have any great attachment to his father, as he was too young to have really felt the loss. It was only in his later years that he said rather sadly, "I wish I had a father when I was growing up."

Both families were in great anticipation of the forthcoming event. Betty was sad and nervous. Henry was happy and in good humor.

/ / / / / / / / / / / / / /

Chapter Fifty-Two
The Birches

The drive upstate brought back some childhood memories to both of them. They reminisced about the times they had spent with their cousins and the German couple who took them into the woods for berry picking and scampering over to Grandma's for her delicious, jarred fruits and Grandpa's workshop where his skills with leather and fabric amazed the children.

They drove up the driveway with the now fully grown birches lining the roadway, tall and stately. Little seemed to have changed over the decades, except for the enlargement of the house with several additions in back and sides. They were greeted warmly by their Aunt Evelyn and rather coldly by Uncle Joseph. Evelyn still showed the signs of her youthful beauty and graciousness, while Joseph seemed smaller and uglier than they had remembered.

They were greeted by a formally dressed butler and ushered into the "salon" or living room as was a more normal name to the visitors. Here they were offered a pre-dinner cocktail which Betty refused and Henry enjoyed. Betty could see that Henry was ready to relish the evening as a social event whereas Betty was all business.

They were soon summoned to the table for the dinner, which proceeded through several courses, accompanied by small tidbits of courtesy conversation. The presence of the butler server mitigated against any serious conversation. Finally, as the coffee and dessert course was reached and Evelyn dismissed the attending butler, the room descended into silence.

Betty broke the silence with one simple request, "Where is my father?"

It took several strained moments, with the added whimpering of Aunt Evelyn, for Joseph to blurt out in startling simplicity, "Oh, he is dead!"

His grossly insensitive manner of the pronouncement just reverberated into the very center of the two siblings' beings. They could barely speak a word. Betty especially was so shocked, hurt, and bereft of any feelings, except loss. The loss was of the years of having a loving father, a friend, and someone whom she had idolized as a child and somehow never gave up hope that one day she might recoup some of the missing love of those lost years. She remembered all the times she had cried out of loneliness and abandonment. Yes, it was true that she was now a grown woman, a mother of two, a wife, with many problems dealing with a sick child. But yet she could not shake off that missing link. The hidden facts nurtured by her Mom merely made her forbearance all the more difficult. He was her Dad, and dammit, she missed him terribly.

As for Henry, as he was to tell her many years later, he never really missed him. In fact, he had no memories of ever being aware of his presence. He did not think that he made any difference in his life at all. She could only think of her loss. She often thought, *"What did he think? Did Martin ever feel regret? Did he ever think of her? How could he blot out the existence of his child, a living human being, who never gave him pain, only love?"* It was this that bothered her so much. How does one give up love so blithely? Sadly she was soon to learn

206

how death deals this blow quickly and yet the love lingers seemingly forever, always present in the undercurrent of living. It is placed at a lower level of consciousness, but never, never goes away.

She soon recovered from her thoughts and faced her uncle.

"And where did he die?"

With some hesitation and a sidelong glance at Evelyn who seemed preoccupied with her own thoughts, he sharply responded, "Oh, in Albany."

It was at this point, that Evelyn raised her eyes and with tears in her eyes and voice, she quietly said, "And we were the only ones in the church."

It was at this point that Betty felt there no longer was any reason to prolong this visit and rose from the table and said that they had to get back home for work and school the next day. There was not even a pretense of urging them to stay. Evelyn walked them to the door and with a curt goodbye, they left.

There was very little conversation on the ride home. Henry merely made small talk about the house, the servants, and the dim memories of their childhood pranks during the few weeks they had spent there for a few summers. Betty related in gruesome details the onerous news they had received. Bart was very understanding and tried to ease Betty's pain by dealing with the practicality.

"I'll go up to Albany and look around in the Hall of Records and try to get some particulars in reference to Martin's life and death."

Bart kept his promise and a few days later, he did just that. He spent several hours in a search and actually contacted the office of the assemblyman who represented the district in which they lived. An

207

office assistant checked the information Bart had retrieved and felt that he had exhausted all available resources.

He then called Betty with the startling news, "Not only didn't Martin die there, but he also never lived there either."

When he returned home they discussed this new turn of events. Betty was not surprised at this new information. She didn't trust Joseph and felt that this was just part of his destructive nature. It was decided that Betty was to call Joseph again and face him with the facts and demand some valid answers. When she did this Joseph was his usual snarling self. Never an apology, not an explanation, just a nervous laugh.

'"Well, we didn't want to distress you." This time he said, "You might look in Tarrytown," and hung up the phone.

The following Saturday, they drove to Tarrytown. Not really knowing how to proceed, Bart said the best bet would be to go to a local store and just ask. They stopped at what used to be called a cigar store, where they sold smokes, newspapers, magazines, candy, etc. He insisted that Betty remain in the car. He knew that this was an emotional trip for her and did not want to expose her to more pain than was needed.

Bart had a wide grin on his face as he returned from the store and related the result of the inquiry.

"Oh yeah, too bad about the Doc. Sure died too young. Nice fella. Loved good Havana cigars. He's buried in the cemetery at St Thomas's. You just continue on this road north until the dead end and then turn left to the entrance. You can't miss it."

"What the blazes does that moniker, Doc, mean?" Betty

screeched.

Bart quietly shrugged his shoulders and said, "Just part of this guy's play acting at life - that's all!"

Betty began to wonder again why Joseph had set them off on a wild chase to Albany, but soon reasoned that he wanted to keep Martin, even in death, wrapped in anonymity as long as he could, to keep his nefarious shenanigans under cover and, also, to keep Martin's life and death hidden, and the longer he could perpetuate this, the better.

/ / / / / / / / / / / / / / /

Chapter Fifty-Three
Death

They reached the stately entrance to the church, found the parish house and elicited the information as to the location of the gravesite. In a carefully manicured portion of the cemetery, they found the grave. Betty clung to Bart's hand in anxiety and strong emotional fears. There was a large oblong horizontally placed tombstone of polished limestone about six feet long. It had no inscription other than the name, LANG, deeply etched into the center of the piece. At the lower left bottom of the stone, in smaller carved letters, it said, "IN PEACE, Martin 1901- 1966." It seemed such a starkly simple statement of a life. Nowhere could you find the rationale for his strangely hidden life, tossed and turned in convolutions of despair, fears, duplicity, and infidelity – no questions asked, none answered. That was still the province of the living. Betty took several photos, noting that this was a double stone. Who was the second occupant to be?

They retraced their path and returned to the store for further inquiry. Once again, Bart entered the store and asked if they could take a look at the home where Doc Lang had lived. When he returned to the car he had a smile and two thumbs up.

They soon were driving up wooded and quiet roads. They soon reached the residence. Strangely and fortuitously, there was a small sign on the front lawn, which indicated that the property was for sale.

"Let's say that we are interested in looking at the house and let me do the talking."

Bart reassured Betty that this ploy was perfect.

/ / / / / / / / / / / / / /

Chapter Fifty-Four

Emilia

They parked the car and went up the steps and rang the bell. In a few moments a rather tall, angular fairly attractive woman opened the door and Bart made his little speech. They entered into a small entrance foyer and then off to one side to a rather large, lavishly decorated living room. Betty gave a sudden hushed gasp as she saw a photo of Martin in an elaborate frame on the mantle, above a working fireplace. The woman, who introduced herself as Mrs. Lang, noticing Betty's reaction, asked whether she knew her husband and Betty, denied any knowledge. She just noted that the photo reminded her of someone. Emilia then took them on a tour of the house.

She then said, "Dr. Lang was very interested in developing new strains of orchids. Would you like to see the greenhouse?"

They looked at one another in amazement. Betty was thinking, *"We were struggling to survive, moving from one smaller home after another and he was developing orchids?"*

Mrs. Lang continued to describe Martin's work and then in a sadder tone said, "He died here of a cerebral hemorrhage. He lived just a few hours after the event. He did not seem to struggle to live."

Bart then asked some financial particulars and they left. They were quiet on the way home.

Suddenly, Bart blurted out, "You should sue the estate!"

Betty said, "What could be our motivation?"

"You could sue for your Mom and the many years of marriage

with no support."

Betty did not feel comfortable with the idea, but then she was not very knowledgeable legally.

Bart said, "Let's tell Henry and Lynda. I'm sure through Henry's business dealings, he must have a lawyer or two whom you could use."

Betty then contacted Henry and he was excited by the fact that Betty and Bart had visited Emilia. He said he would go to visit her and tell her the truth about Martin and his hidden family. He also agreed to sue the estate. A lawyer was retained and a large sum was to be asked for Stella only.

Henry decided to visit Emilia, without prior notice.

On a quiet Sunday afternoon, he rang the bell and Emilia opened the door and without any preparation, he stated, "I am Henry Lang, Martin's son, and the couple who came to look at the house was my sister, Betty and her husband, Bart."

Emilia's reaction was immediate.

"I knew it, I knew it," she cried. "I knew there was something in his life that was kept from me. Why? Why didn't he tell me? Didn't he know that I would have loved you all as I loved him? Why did he deny this joy for me, too?"

She was so distraught, she looked ready to collapse. Henry assisted her to a chair. She urged him to take the photo from the mantle.

"You look just like him. Please take it. I have others."

That photo sits on the author's desk as these words are written.

Henry then said, "I really think there is more to this story of which you are not aware. I don't know the details, but I think a member of the family is involved. I do not want to accuse anyone as I do not have all the facts."

It took a few more minutes until she recovered from the shock. She then pressed Henry for information about their families. He was happy to fill in the blanks. She thanked him for opening the book into Martin's life. He did not indicate that there was to be a lawsuit. He left with really no intention of returning.

Her sadness was immediately followed by a burst of anger. She knew who the perpetrator was. What she did not know or even have a glimmer of an idea was what the reasons for his actions were. She dialed Joseph's number. Evie answered and she asked to speak to Joe, without any conversation with Evie, which was unusual.

"Hi Emmy, How are you?"

"I am not in the mood for small talk. Henry came to see me today and I need to talk to you at once."

"I'll be there in a short while."

He hung up the phone and sat for a while thinking. *A plan, I need a plan...* he thought. Evie sensed something had happened and did not interfere. Joseph tried to keep his anxiety at a low level, hoping to dissuade Emilia from any further inquiry as to this new wrinkle in the saga of Martin.

As he rang the bell, he put on his smiling face.

"Hi, Emmy."

She merely nodded in response. They went into the kitchen as she had made a pot of tea which they quietly drank. Emelia finally broke the silence.

214

"Well?" she demanded.

Joseph reasoned that it was simpler to put the blame on Martin, who could not refute his assertions.

"Martin was not happy in his marriage and they separated. It was Stella's wish that he sever contact with the children and find somewhere else to live. It is as simple as that. Really nothing to be agitated about. We shall continue our lives as before. I certainly will help you find a small apartment wherever you choose to live."

Emmy was not really satisfied with Joseph's explanation, as it did not fit his character of quiet divisive diplomacy. She felt that something was missing. Unfortunately, she didn't have a clue as to a possible resource to find the truth. She felt boxed in and knew that the true story was hidden with Martin in his coffin.

She thanked Joseph for coming so quickly and said she would try to put the events of the day out of her mind. She did not think she would ever see those people again.

/ / / / / / / / / / / / / / / /

Chapter Fifty-Five

Litigation

The lawyers in their searching discovered that Martin's Will, indicated that the entire estate went to Emilia, with this comment *"Whether she be my wife or not at the time of my death."* It was this phrase, which prompted further investigation and they came up empty as there was no evidence of a marriage between the two parties.

Papers were delivered to Emilia in Stella's name indicating the suit against Martin's estate. Emmy immediately called Joseph and he reassured her that nothing would come of it and not to be upset. His anger against Betty reached such a pitch that Evie had to leave the house. She just couldn't tolerate his screaming and attacks against her brother's children. Joseph called Betty and began a tirade of threats.

She waited silently and finally said, "Uncle Joseph, I am not a child, you no longer can intimidate me. I am well aware of your illegal activities and if I choose to engage in your game, I easily could. However, I am not cut from the same cloth as you, so I will not threaten you. The suit against my father's estate is proper and legal. You have no input in this matter. If you have nothing of importance to tell me, this conversation has ended."

Joseph responded, "I warn you to leave Emilia alone." With that he hung up.

The lawyers were told by Emilia to send the papers to Joseph. Within a month, Stella received a check signed by Emmy, but the funds came from Joseph's bank.

Afterword

Although the basis of the characters depicted in these pages comes from real life, many of the incidents were fabricated to move the story along. As of this writing (2016), most of the personae are deceased. I hesitated publishing this story earlier as I didn't want to expose a family's dirty linen. However, I needed to write the story because of the pain in my life time.

Much still remains unknown. There are many unanswered questions. The author remains to this day (2016) more than fifty years after Martin's death still wondering why this man chose the path he took. The lingering thought returns to the several diabetic comas he endured and whether this repeated assault on his system may have caused some deterioration in brain processes. This seems to be circumstantially related to the cause of death itself.

We shall never know. We can only assume...the truth lies hidden with Martin.

Acknowledgements

My thanks and gratitude to all of my friends and family who encouraged me to undertake the responsibility of putting these words to paper. As is evident, I am not a professional writer. However, I decided to write this story, because as some professional writers say, *"I had to."* A very special thanks goes to Carol Chiani* for the many hours spent at the computer designing the format, scanning the photos, and helping me through some of the unimaginable processes needed to effect this small volume. She did all this under much physical stress and often bringing food for our lunches. My appreciative thanks go to all the Hunter Gals who were always ready with a smile and an answer to many questions. A special kudo to Susan Bellido for her patience and skills in finally helping us finish the first draft of this book. Of course, a deep sense of gratitude goes to the staff at the American Lung Association, Northeastern region, especially Kristin and Serena, in establishing the Research Fund in my daughter Karen's name. Very special thanks to Susan Cole, who at Oxford University in the summer of 2011 urged me to complete this book. And then, of course, a profound appreciation of Katrina Amaro's artistic know-how in designing some of the material which enhanced the final product. Last, but certainly not least, my special thanks to Charlotte Adomaitis for her gracious professionalism in providing her knowledge and skills to complete the herculean editing task. Of all those still unnamed, but whose influence is deeply felt, my thanks. You all have made the sadness in my life so much easier to bear.

The Front Cover: Although the original photos were taken by the author one summer at Oxford University, the arrangement for printing was the work of a wonderful woman whose computer graphic skills were outstanding. Sadly, she died of complications of kidney dysfunction in December, 2015. We all shall miss her.

Credits

<u>Front Cover</u>:   Photo by Bea Klier at Oxford University; Design by Carol Chiani

<u>Page 172</u>: Author's photo at 99th Birthday Party by Sue Kelly

<u>Back Cover</u>: Author's photo by Jim Mukerjee, Paris 2014

<u>Final Covers</u>: Charles Levine

<u>Family Photos</u>: Photographers unknown

<u>Editing</u>: Charlotte Adomaitis

<u>Publisher</u>: Amazon.com CreateSpace

Finis

Meet the Author

99TH Birthday Pic

Bea Klier was educated in the NYC schools, including Hunter College from which she graduated in 1937 with a degree in geology. As she was female and no safety net existed at that time, she worked at several stop gap jobs to help her mother and younger brother. In 1941, she married and went to work as a meteorologist (civilian) for the Air Force Research and Development Division in New Jersey. When her husband was relocated to New York and found housing at Fort Jay (Governor's Island), she left the weather station and went to work for a company which was developing mobile radar units for deployment in the South Pacific theater of war. She had two children and was a stay at home mom for ten years, as her younger child was born ill and died at thirty. She taught Geological Sciences in the public schools in New

York City. She did Climatological Research at NASA and eventually went to work for a major science organization. She joined the Amateur Astronomer's Association and built her own 8-inch reflector telescope. After many years as an educator, she left to pursue other avenues of interest. Among these were traveling on river boats, following total solar eclipses, and riding on trains on any continent. Someone suggested that she write about some of her adventures. Thus began her interest in writing. This is her first book. There are two more in the pipeline. Bea is 99 this year and lives in Forest Hills.

Made in the USA
Middletown, DE
06 February 2017